Disintegral

Thiago,

Enjoy the book!

Disintegral

Kyle Styron

Library of Congress Control Number:		2014915297
ISBN:	Hardcover	978-1-4990-6549-7
	Softcover	978-1-4990-6550-3
	eBook	978-1-4990-6548-0

This is a work of fiction. Names, characters, places and incidents either are the product of the author's imagination or are used fictitiously, and any resemblance to any actual persons, living or dead, events, or locales is entirely coincidental.

This book was printed in the United States of America.

Rev. date: 09/02/2014

To order additional copies of this book, contact:
Xlibris LLC
1-888-795-4274
www.Xlibris.com
Orders@Xlibris.com
539501

We knew the world would not be the same. Few people laughed, few people cried, most people were silent. I remembered the line from the Hindu scripture, the ***Bhagavad-Gita.*** Vishnu is trying to persuade the Prince that he should do his duty and to impress him takes on his multi-armed form and says, "Now I am become Death, the destroyer of worlds." I suppose we all thought that, one way or another.

—Robert Oppenheimer

Man's respect for the imponderables varies according to his mental constitution and environment. Through certain modes of thought and training, it can be elevated tremendously, yet there is always a limit.

—H.P. Lovecraft

"Miserable! . . . What mean you, foolish girl? Dost thou deem it misery to be endowed with marvelous gifts, against which no power nor strength could avail an enemy? Misery, to be able to quell the mightiest with a breath? Misery, to be as terrible as thou art beautiful? Woudst thou, then, have preferred the condition of a weak woman, exposed to all evil and capable of none?"

—Nathaniel Hawthorne, Rappaccini's Daughter

Dedication

This novel is culled from so much of my personal experiences and depicts a radically fictionalized version of unpleasant events from the past. The individuals who inspired me in this effort include Brian Alessandro, the Russian, Ricardo Carmona, Craig Byrne, Mom, Dad, Randy, David Lynch, John Carpenter, and David Cronenberg.

Prologue
The New Journal

From the Journal of Chester Syme

January 1, 2003

I did this before, and it was pointless. I wrote pages and pages, day after day, and it became a chore. In short, a new journal is a lousy Christmas gift.

I gave my friend Roger a much better gift in return last week. I bought him Jed Haele's canon of two novels: ***Shelby*** and ***Dance of the Damned***. Not only did Roger groan over a literary gift ("Reading is too much work!"), but also complained that I wasted sixty dollars on something I could have just printed out from my own computer.

I guess the latter is a logical criticism from his perspective, but he doesn't understand the process. Jed distributes the novels through his website. After you purchase them, he e-mails the text to you, and you print it out for your own use. All or many of Jed Haele's subscribers (there are more than 1,800 of us) could get together and pay for just one subscription and share them. This would be legal because he doesn't copyright his novels. However, Jed does not need to do so. The majority of his fans understand that such tactics would force him to seek legal protection and pay hard copy publishers. This is a concern expressed on many of the message boards and websites that cover Jed Haele's novels. I am not aware of any website that contains pirate versions of his texts. I've tried all of the ordinary Internet search options, as well as some unconventional ones. This does not surprise me at all, because his fans understand this point well. The continued integrity of his fiction (i.e., its content) depends upon our individual integrity. We are all accountable.

(Later)

Of course, I must concede that it will happen. What's important is that this is not a common tactic. Most of the readers behave.

January 10, 2003

Okay. Let's re-start. My name is Chester Syme. I'm a senior at Dog Crap University in Queens. My major is horseshit, and next semester I am taking three courses toward that major: Donkey Fart, Cat Piss, and Dog Puke.

Ugh! You'll have to excuse me, but my school is so lame! I am too embarrassed to name names even in my own journal. The choice to go there is the saddest concession of my life so far.

I have to go back to school on Monday. This semester is my last semester. That means that I have to look for a job (that would "ideally" start the day after graduation, of course) in addition to the term papers and exams. That Dog Puke final exam with Professor Bally and thesis required by Professor Rexic for Cat Piss are legendary. In this newfangled hell on earth, I will be more depressed than usual.

January 17, 2003

Ugh! This stupid book. I hate it! What a lousy gift!

I guess some people garner solace from a journal. They place their thoughts down on paper, and it's said. They've expressed all of their longing, anger, bitterness, etc. I consider this notion toothless. Expression on the page accomplishes nothing at all! It may be a mild opiate, but the pain remains.

Rather, I choose to face my "newfangled hell on earth" sober. It is how it is, and I will not patronize my reality by crapping and whining down the page! There are two kinds of people in this world. There are those who rip the bandage off in one quick tear, and those who slowly and painfully pry it away from their skin. I rip it off!

February 8, 2003

Roger finally finished the novels. We talked about them for hours. Well, an hour. He loved how Jed finally reveals the futuristic setting of ***Dance of the Damned*** in the section where Andrew, who's a terminally ill teenager with unlimited resources, has his dick pulled from the freezer and re-attached following three weeks of life as a teenage girl. "Such advances in technology! Wow! I didn't see it coming," he said.

Sharing the two novels with Roger wasn't as much fun as I expected. I figured that it would be neat to have a live person with whom I could discuss Jed Haele. It was mildly satisfying, but the victory was pyrrhic. Roger didn't understand the books, and the insights he threw back at me once I explained them weren't novel or provocative enough. The worst of it is that he said he wouldn't bother with the third novel.

The third novel! Jed's second novel, ***Dance of the Damned***, ends so brilliantly. As its protagonist lies dying, a serum is discovered that could have saved him, but his body is so ravaged that he cannot be saved. I am shuddering with anticipation for the follow-up.

I did the standard check of all the spoiler sites yet again today, and the only one with any information about the third novel is Jerry's site. He claimed that the plot involves a split personality. "There's a character who is a holier–than-thou born-again Christian by day and a whoring heroin addict by night," he posted. That is a questionable leak, because Jed is cleverer than that. I know that this book will not be clichéd and patronizing. It will be ferocious and raw, just like ***Shelby*** and ***Dance of the Damned***. His characters' quirks spring from plausible plot twists.

The sources for most Jed Haele spoilers usually allege that they've eavesdropped on him at the nightclubs he frequents in the East Village. I've seen them in action. This cult of vipers lurks in the corners and shadows of his favorite nightspots. However, when I speak to the "cult of vipers" after he leaves, they know nothing.

Besides, I could have read the book by now if I wanted to. I know where he lives, and that he handwrites the novels. I will wait, blissfully. One day a brand-new, thick, and consistently surprising novel will arrive in my e-mail inbox. That's what I want.

I won't read those drafts, and I know that the spoilers get most of it wrong. Half of the fun of ***Dance of the Damned*** was comparing the speculation on the Internet (which was sporadically peppered with good leaks) to the finished product. For instance, one web site correctly discovered that the plot involved a sex change. However, they speculated that Andrew dies on the operating table, and that the final scene is his funeral, where he is dressed as a girl. There's a line in the book where he says, "I want to die as a female, because they live longer statistically speaking," and I suspect that Jed must have thrown that line around at a cocktail party as a joke, and a member of the "cult of vipers" extrapolated a plot thread from the remark.

February 9, 2003

I think that I can get into this now, because I enjoy writing about Jed Haele. That's contrary to the premise of a journal (i.e., a document of one's ongoing stream of consciousness whenever one sees fit to place said consciousness on the page that generally concerns one's life and times.) On the other hand, it is in accord with the most important rule for writing a journal (i.e., There are no rules. Write whatever the hell you want!), so we'll see where this goes.

Let me preface this by saying that I'm straight. Okay? With that said, I think Jed is hot. He's lanky, with brown hair dyed dirty blond, and avocado green eyes. He frequently makes tongue gestures, but they aren't crass. They're cute. He rolls it, and licks his lips with that candy red appendage. He is the only man with whom I could have sex, and I would go all the way. Yes, I would do that.

He has unique taste, and that flavor penetrates his novels. His novel ***Shelby*** commences with an extended monologue by the character Masha. She struts (most of his characters strut) down Queens Boulevard in the middle of a weekday on her way to meet Shelby. She makes a series of aggressive phone calls while smoking and lapses into Russian when she's mad. By page two, you know that she is the most bitter and relentless character in the novel. Half of the first page is in Russian. Then the novel introduces us to Shelby: "Masha knocked with her distended knuckles. The door opened, and Shelby stood there." That's on page five. The chapter ends on that line, and Shelby is absent for most of the rest of the novel. It's like Bram Stoker's ***Dracula,*** where the titular character only plays a supporting role page for page, but the reader feels his presence throughout.

Part 1

The Destroyer

From the Journals of Shane Lasch

May 22, 2003

When I talk to Justin about Hunter, it always unfolds like a rerun. The conversation starts after work once we've had a few drinks. He drolly asks, "Why," and I know he's referring to the "relationship."

"You're right. She has been a miscalculation since day one," I admit.

Today, he was neurotically handling his already messed up hair so much that I wanted to get him a hair net.

"How so?" he asked in response.

"She was initially a sport fuck." He laughed. I groaned and continued. "When I met her in L.A. last year I was on vacation and she was shooting." I paused.

"She was shooting porn."

"Yeah, it was porn," I said grimly. "She used to be a legit actress, but got older, and she switched to porn."

He laughed again, harder. I grinned and added, "Probably soft-core, because I only rent and buy hardcore." He nodded, as if to say "Duh."

"It was enticing, and then she followed me to New York." I paused and sighed hard. "Who am I to turn her down? Considering her age and lifestyle, she is still remarkably hot."

"If you know what's good for you," he said, leaning back, relaxed. "What's up this weekend?" he asked, signaling the waitress for another cocktail.

"The holiday weekend? Well, Hunter. She . . ." I trailed off.

"You should read a book. There's this writer I want to recommend to you. He's really good. . ." I tuned him out while he went on. When I continued listening, he was thankfully no longer interested in discussing Hunter, my weekend plans, or his new favorite novelist.

May 26, 2003

Drug dealers are twitchy and paranoid. I hate them. I'm sure that they die from strokes or heart attacks, because they are primed to explode. I guess it's a hazard of the trade, as they are always on edge about getting busted or attacked by their clientele.

Hunter introduced me to this dealer she's "friends with" named Cecil on Saturday. When he answered the door to his cramped basement apartment, I couldn't help but laugh. He was pale with greasy overgrown dreadlocks and a perpetually vibrating lip. Hunter stepped on my toe with her stiletto heel so forcefully that it made a deep indentation in the leather. This shut me up nicely.

A couple of minutes later, when he went to gather her purchase from a valise across the room, she drew close to me on the surprisingly clean sofa. "You know how dealers are," She explained. "The slightest thing provokes them."

"Such as laughing in their face?" I suggested.

She withdrew and lowered her voice. "Something just like that, and he might shoot you." This was her last sober exchange of the three-day weekend.

While Hunter was shooting up, Cecil went to puke in his tiny bathroom without closing the door. She fell back smiling. His retching was alarmingly loud, and Hunter giggled as she aped the noise. "Yack, yack."

That was Saturday. Somehow I peeled her off the couch much later that evening and brought her to my apartment, where I didn't fuck her. Maybe it was because I would have felt guilty afterward, or because I was afraid she contracted something from the syringe she used, or because she looked horrible and I knew she would probably throw up on me, projectile style, in the midst of the act.

On Sunday, Hunter's friend Sharisse came by the apartment unannounced, and the girls did some baking. I couldn't help but partake, as pot laced baked goods do not involve needle use, and they make a good accompaniment to ***The Simpsons***. I pulled out my DVD and watched episodes of the show until I fell asleep.

She finished the remaining brownies as I woke up this morning. Blackish grimy crumbs stained her stubbed fingers. Mine felt soft, but smelled grungy since I had licked them clean hours earlier. She mumbled something about going to Rockaway Beach with her mouth full, and I grunted a negative answer.

"Sure?" she asked.

My first words of the day: "Sunlight. Just won't work for me today."

She licked her fingers clean and got dressed. "See you when I see you?" she asked, maybe a half hour later.

"Don't be like that."

"Why not?"

"I'm hung over, and you should be too," I scoffed.

She flung her overnight bag over her shoulder. "While you were sleeping, I snagged some towels."

"Not the $100 bill towel?"

She opened her bag and yanked out a towel that looked like my $100 bill towel. "Actually I took two towels. One for me and your favorite towel as well. It was wishful thinking."

She bopped around neurotically, checking to see if she had left anything she wanted to take with her to the beach and left a few minutes later without saying anything else.

Our relationship has degenerated into this. It's an awkward hostility in that it comes from both of us, like a bouncing ball that we throw back and forth.

I will not mourn the end of the relationship. I know that her heroin addiction will get increasingly hopeless, and I dread the final stages. I am eager to get that worry out of my life.

A few hours later, I finally gathered enough energy and sat up. I stumbled a bit on my way to the kitchenette and glared at the dirty dishes the girls left for me to clean. My philosophy is if you're a guest in someone's house and make a mess while using their dishes, you should clean them. I clean the dishes that I use when I'm a guest. This surprises people, but I always insist.

I did not feel like cleaning my guest's dirty dishes and pondered the narcotic effects of the crud lining my mixing bowl. Instead, I dressed and left my apartment.

I took the E train to Midtown, with no specific destination in mind, and decided en route to spend my paid holiday shopping with the tourists in Times Square. I was nauseous by the time I got off the train, but had lunch anyway in a food court that served diner-quality burgers. I felt fine after I ate and realized I had felt ill earlier from not eating for so long. It's easy to confuse prolonged hunger nausea from the "about to puke" sort. That used to be such a problem for me.

Next up was the multilevel music store. The street level was crowded, so I wandered downstairs. They kept the classical music, show tunes, and country Western CDs on this more somber level.

What were they thinking? If they display such crap in the basement, then not only is it more likely to be a graveyard, but the resulting isolation will attract transients and perverts.

Just as I was thinking this, two tourists from the Bible belt broke into a fight. Initially I thought the first hillbilly (we'll pretend his name is Roy) was drunk and that the second (let's call him Buck) got in his way. Roy was perusing the Travis Tritt CDs when Buck came from upstairs and headed straight for the country section. Two aisles over, I hunted through the New Age CDs in pursuit of an Enya import.

I still hadn't found it when Roy raised his arm to deliver a blow to the back of Buck's head in a weirdly hesitant slow motion that belied the aggressive anger on his face. His beefy flannel-clad arm was unexpectedly reluctant, but it did its job. The impact made a squishy thud. Then Buck hollered something incomprehensible in his backwoods dialect.

The only other person on that level sped down the aisle between the hillbillies and me. He didn't notice the confrontation, or maybe he was just afraid of being around a fight since he walked away fast like a wimp. He turned his head for a split second and winked at me when he passed. As I said, this empty floor would only attract creeps.

I continued my search for the ever-elusive Enya import, since the fight subsided just as quickly as it began. They resumed browsing as if nothing had happened.

Then I went to the bar in the stupid multilevel arcade (What is the deal with all these multilevel stores in Manhattan?). My beer and vodka shots passed by unremarkably as I watched the following patrons at the bar: grim street people guzzling cheap beer, Euro-trash tourists waiting for their vacation to become fun, teenage tourists from Middle America who probably squandered half their stay in order to procure fake IDs only to see that half-priced drinks are still too fucking expensive, not too much borough trash, some cretin with purple hair who only drank Budweiser, and at the end a very lonely middle-aged lady drinking a glass of white wine, probably the only one ever served at that bar, who obviously walked into the wrong place. When I contemplated switching to tequila shots, I noticed it was now dark outside. It was time to go home.

Here I am writing about my boring day at 3:00 a.m. on Tuesday the twenty-seventh, unable to sleep. Yes, my insomnia is still hell on earth. I eliminated caffeine after 3:00 p.m. It's been two weeks of agony now, with no results. Maybe 2:00 p.m.?

May 27, 2003

I had a freaky dream last night. I was walking to my parents' house, as if I still lived there, and a cold wind blew over me. As I made my way around a winding downward sloping hill, it became stronger and stronger. The Stop sign ahead of me shimmied. Each footstep was more difficult. My calves and thigh muscles pulsed. The winds increased to what seemed like hurricane force, and the Stop sign slipped off the post and flew toward me.

I was now out of my body and saw that I wasn't wearing a hat. The sign sliced through my skull. The cut was clean through the top third of my head, just above my eyes. Five feet and nine inches of me fell back on the ground. The other three inches flew back a few yards, and that hat-covered dome landed in some hedges.

Everything stopped, the wind and my heart. There was no blood for a brief moment. Then, it flowed out to form a rapidly expanding stream down the hill.

That image fucked me up all day! I went to work and, at one point, stared at the monitor for half an hour. I replayed the image of blood draining from my skull onto the pavement repeatedly. I didn't eat lunch. Instead, I drank my lunch and dinner with Justin after work. He eyed some chicks while I told him about my dream. I grimaced. "C'mon, bub. Listen to me!" I pleaded.

He rolled his eyes. "They're hot. Man!"

"Justin, you're coming off a long weekend. Can't you keep it in your pants for like an hour so we can talk about this?"

He grinned. "You should have come. There was an abundance of fresh and clean eighteen-year-old ass waiting to get popped."

Eighteen-year-old virgins? As if, I thought, but instead I said, "What you don't understand, Justin, is that this scared the shit out of me."

"How infantile." He cackled at his "clever line" and took a sloppy swig of his beer. It dribbled down his chin. I gave him my evil eye, and he sighed. "Ugh! So what happened again?" he asked with absolutely no enthusiasm. I described it a second time. "Whoa. That's intense and brief. Are you sure that there wasn't an earlier part that you don't remember? My dreams are usually more involved than that."

I really didn't know how to respond to that. "It was enough," I said. Justin's comment made me think hard, but I came up with nothing. I read somewhere once that we all dream every night but only remember small fragments. Who knows where my mind could have wandered? I could have died ten other ways for all I know. I have probably dreamed of much more grisly deaths, but I just don't remember them.

Still, they are only dreams. The anxiety, which my nightmare provoked, has faded away. I think that writing about this bad dream has sped up the process. I once read that the body produces chemical anesthetics called endorphins when one sustains physical trauma. I suspect that there are emotional endorphins, which naturally ease the sadness. Possibly, writing is a catalyst for these mental opiates. I think that's why I write so much in this journal.

May 28, 2003
3:30 p.m.

Hunter called me at work this morning. She blew off a shoot. "You're a bad girl!" I grumbled.

"They recast the guy I was going to do the scene with, and he's a sleaze. I worked with him on another film in January, and he was filthy. He tried to . . . well, do something that they weren't paying for that day."

"Yikes."

"You sound hoarse. Did you go out last night?" she asked.

"Without you? Never." Why shouldn't I lie to her at this point? "Are you with Sharisse?" I asked.

"Yeah. Why don't you get out of work early?" she asked. She continued to nag me for a few minutes while I aimlessly surfed the net and tuned her out. "Serious fucking bastard," she said and then sighed too dramatically.

"Are you kidding me? I could care less about this . . ." The sound of shuffling footsteps coming toward my cubicle startled me. I stuttered some syllables as I grasped for convincing workplace dialogue. "I'll fax the transcript ASAP, sir, and then I'll . . ." I trailed off. He passed without looking or speaking to me and left the office. "Sorry, babe."

"Was it Carly?"

"No, it was her assistant."

"The guy who limps like that guy in 'The Usual Suspects'? The lurking freak? The one who cruises all the hot piece of ass guys in the office?"

"Yep, that freak. Except he didn't lurk today, or try to engage me in conversation. I think he left for the day, actually. Charlene is wherever."

"So the big boss lady and her limping assistant are now gone. Oh yeah, and it is Friday."

"It is Friday," I said grimly.

She giggled. "En route get a big bag of tortilla chips."

I sighed. I'm writing this on the train because one day when I'm older and serious, I want proof that I was once a slacker. No one will believe it if I wind up being half as boring as my parents.

(Much Later . . . As I'm sobering up!)

My evening was somewhat more interesting than I expected. Here's a summary: I went to Buy N' Go and met an acquaintance from college, and he was working there! Then, I went to Sharisse's little house and held a gun for the very first time! After that, we drove to Rockaway Beach in the middle of the night for target practice with beer cans!

I procured a bag of blue corn chips rather easily in the eerily quiet and brightly lit store. One could peacefully sashay down the aisles for hours. I browsed the endless selection of power protein low-carb fiber-rich vitamin laced NutraSweet and aspartame-filled Franken-food bars. This was where I encountered the only other soul besides the creepy and overly pierced cashier who flirted with me when I checked out.

Jeremiah, a psychology major and winner of a silver medal at commencement, was re-stocking cans of powdered diet food and wearing a bright yellow polo shirt with a nametag. I hated him back in school (I won bronze. That motherfucker!) but concealed my amusement. "You didn't get a job?" I asked. "It's a shame."

He looked up from the box of nutrient-enriched chocolate mousse shake cans and stared at be blankly. "I have a job," he said soberly.

I think the world is better off with one less mind-fucker, I thought to myself. Instead, I said "I think the world is worse off with one less psychologist."

"Yeah, I guess so," he said weakly and frowned.

OK. I was a jerk, but this guy had the audacity to deconstruct me one day a few years ago over lunch with a mutual friend of ours. I wrote about that conversation in my journal before. I'm going to fish through my old journals and find what I wrote about it. It was during the spring 2001 semester of my junior year, if my memory serves me. I'm interested in seeing what I wrote that day, because for the life of me I don't understand why Caleb (the mutual friend) would have introduced me to a jerk like that.

I hadn't spoken to Caleb since graduation, so I rang him up once I got to Sharisse's house in Howard Beach this afternoon (which she inherited from her dad, who died from cancer that a blood pressure medicine induced. He received a settlement from a class-action suit of well over a half million. The check arrived six weeks after he succumbed last year, and I would guesstimate she's pissed away at least half of it so far.) Sharisse smiled at me with her bloodshot gray eyes as I dialed in her kitchen. "Who you calling, hunny?" Sharisse asked.

"I'm nobody's hunny, little missy Anne," I said gruffly.

"No, you ain't, Mr. Lasch," she grunted and rejoined her rambunctious friends in her living room. Hunter emerged immediately after Sharisse left, as if they were a tag team. I held up the garish large bag of blue corn tortilla chips and ripped it open while the line rang. "I'm calling Caleb," I said to Hunter.

She laughed. "That's a blast from the past."

"I told you about Caleb?" I asked.

She nodded. "He's one of the college buddies that you introduced me to when I moved here with . . ."

He picked up, and I shushed her. "Hey, Caleb."

"Who are you?"

"Shane. You know, from school."

"College?"

"Yeah. We ate lunch together that year when you were a Finance major."

"Oh! Right? Right. Right. Right. Hey, Kala. It's Lasch on the phone."

"You're still with her?"

"Yeah, dude."

"Oh. That's cool."

"Yeah. Did you graduate yet?"

"Yeah. In January."

"What are you doing?"

"I'm working with my dad."

"That sucks." I paused. "I ran into Jeremiah today."

"That jerk-off?"

"Yeah. What happened to him? He's working at Buy N' Go."

"Yeah. He's a stock boy." I laughed and then he laughed with me at him. "I haven't spoken to him since school. A while back I went to Buy N' Go and he was my cashier," he said and laughed some more.

"No shit?"

"No shit, dude."

Hunter growled and tugged at her tank top. "Got to go, man. The natives are getting restless here. We have to hang out one day soon. Nice talking to you. Bye."

Hunter made nachos, and one of Sharisse's men made us margaritas. We watched some grade B and C action movies that Sharisse's other man rented from the video store.

Tim and Marvin are bartenders, and this was the third or fourth time I hung out with them. I still mixed up their names. One is shorter and stockier than the other is. I'm pretty sure that his name is Marvin. The other is tall and quite homely. He is Tim, I think.

It's amusing, because even now that I'm all grown-up I still find that I'm the youngest person in the room. Sharisse is closer to thirty, and the butch bartenders with really deep voices are over thirty. Of course, Hunter will be twenty-eight next month. Shari's other friend, Clea, is closer to my age, but she went to prison for corrupting a minor, served three years and hasn't aged well.

The gun came out while we were watching a C or maybe even D quality shoot-em-up with no recognizable faces except for this guy who had a laugh-free sitcom like three years ago. Marvin, who picked up the films, really enjoyed the action. He aped as if he had a machine gun during the hard-core sequences and built up quite a sweat during the third reel.

While the credits rolled, Clea went to another room and returned with a shoebox. Sharisse was slumped into a recliner by the window, almost asleep. "Shari! Babe!" Clea hollered. Sharisse sprung up, looked at the box in Clea's hand, and shook her head. Clea dismissively waved her free arm. "The boys will like it," she said.

"What?" Marvin asked.

Clea opened up the box and pulled out a slender, sleek gun. It fit her small ladylike hands very nicely. Marvin grinned, but Clea turned to me. "I think Shane would look better holding it."

Hunter looked up from her tame stupor. "No, Clea. Shane . . ." She paused and glanced at me. "You should be careful with the quiet ones," she said ominously.

Clea shook her head. "I've been locked down, Hunter. I needed to be a good judge of character to survive in jail, and I still am." She grinned at me. "Get your ass over here, Shane." I complied, and she handed me the gun. She snuggled behind me and held my arms up to guide them. We faced the kitchen. "Aim for the clock." She pulled my arms up by a slight angle and held me still. The smooth gun became heavy in my hands. "You could take out the clock if you aim it like this." She released my arms now, and I abruptly turned around. I dropped my arms and held it with my left hand. "Is it loaded?" I asked.

"Um, no," she scoffed.

"Cool!" I twirled it around and pointed it at everyone just as she showed me.

Hunter lunged from her chair and pinned me face down on the wood floor. Everyone laughed when I overpowered her and wound up on top, pointing the gun at her chest. I chuckled. "Babe, it's not loaded. Didn't you hear her?"

"It's still not cool, Shane," she said weakly.

"Okay, whatever."

Then we drove to the beach, because I wanted to shoot the gun for real. It was so late, and I correctly figured that no one would be there. We bought two cases of beer along the way and I giddily anticipated my late-night target practice. Clea decided we should make it a game.

Clea, Marvin, and I each got six shots. While Sharisse and Hunter restarted the remnants of a small fire that some kids likely let go out earlier, Clea loaded the gun in the darkness. Tim fucked around by the shore, getting himself drenched in the waves for no apparent reason.

"What's up with him?" I asked.

"He doesn't like guns, and he's fucking insane."

"Yeah. Isn't he going to be cold?"

Clea shook her head and spun the chamber. "Are you boys ready?" she asked.

Sharisse, Tim, and Hunter cheered on their respective partners with each round. Clea threw six cans in the air and shot into the cloudy night sky. Each time, she hit the can. It sprayed a foamy spark across the sky like a firecracker.

Marvin gave up after five. I also failed but didn't give up. My aim was all right, but my night vision isn't acute enough. I came closer with each can. I threw the sixth can at a ninety-degree angle, knelt down, and aimed in the same direction.

The girls laughed. "You missed again!" Hunter yelled playfully.

"You don't think I can do better, dear?"

She frowned and handed me another can. "Give it a shot."

I held the sweating can for a few extra moments. "Lucky seven. Lucky seven. Lucky seven!" Clea and Sharisse chanted faster and faster as I idled.

"We'll see." I threw it hard and swirled my gun about in the air. Once the can reached its apex and began its descent, I pulled the trigger. It fell to the sand without a scratch.

"That's a wrap," Tim said. He was still soaked but didn't shiver at all.

Tim went home, and Marvin and I retrieved the cans from the sand around us. The top of one of the cans had a slight puncture because it had landed on a broken shell. The beer leaked into the sand. The other twelve were still intact.

The girls lined up and opened their cans first and knowingly gave themselves wet T-shirts. They leisurely enjoyed their beers on the damp sand. I abstained initially, but once the girls drank a few they got rowdy, so I nursed one to calm my nerves. Then Marvin produced a bottle of whiskey, and I drank for real.

God. I have to get away from these people. By dawn, I was "about to puke" nauseous, and Clea, who still hoards her cigarettes as if the outside world also operates on a barter system, was shooting blanks into the ocean. Ugh. I have to make some new friends. All this Queens white trash is getting old. Real old.

May 29, 2003

Nothing much happened today aside from some annoying phone calls from Hunter, but I dug up that old journal where I wrote about Jeremiah. This excerpt is dated March 8, 2001, and based on the text, you can tell it's a Friday:

Caleb is a creep. I hate it when cowardly schmucks try to criticize you by using another person. He did this today, because he wanted to tell me he thinks I'm a cold and unpleasant egomaniac.

We had our Investment Finance midterm today. Afterward, we ate Mexican take-out with beer for lunch with this guy named Jeremiah Rogers on the big lawn. His name was familiar, and I realized he writes an advice column for one of the universities' papers. He stuffed his face for maybe thirty seconds before he started in on me. I want to emphasize that all we had said to each other at this point was "Hi."

"You have a very aggressive personality. I've heard that you enjoy killing the curve. You deliberately do well so that others fail," he said. Then, he ate a taco in thirty seconds flat, intending this to serve as a dramatic pause. "That's not a very nice thing for you to do. You're only hurting yourself. After all, you can't ride into battle at the front of the pack on a white horse and not expect to be shot at." I chewed slowly. My disgust simmered just like a pot of slow-cooking chili that's starting to burn. He inhaled another taco. "After all, Shane, there's more to life than being the best. If that's your focus, then you will wind up alone. There will never be time for anyone else. Can't you see that this behavior pattern is exceptionally self-centered? You'll become a deviant."

I spit a big mouthful of partially chewed taco onto his shirt. "You don't know me. How dare you!" I would have slammed my fist into his jaw, but Caleb put his beer down on the grass and grabbed me just as I lunged. I'm not sure if Jeremiah was frightened. He just remarked, "This is what I'm talking about," and calmly walked away. I continued to thrash around, but Caleb held me down. Once I had relaxed, he said he was sorry for what had happened.

This is how I knew Jeremiah was speaking for Caleb. Caleb knew how I would react and prepared Jeremiah for it. Caleb is strong, but not too bright. He can't be eloquent, and stutters. He needed Jeremiah to speak for him.

I hate being on the outside like this. I always feel that people are putting on a false front to me, and that when I'm not around they are frank, honest, and sincere. I don't trust any of my friends.

I'm glad that it's 2003 now. I believe that I'm less paranoid and more stable these days. I have a great job. Justin and Constance are great friends, and I trust them. Hunter is a problem, but that's not going to last much longer. I'm probably going to dump her shortly after her birthday on the fifteenth. After that, I'll find a nice girl, and we'll have a long-term relationship. I think that the above re-printed passage shows an earlier model of Shane Lasch. The current model still has flaws, but it is much improved.

May 30, 2003

I witnessed another fight today. This time it was on a train, but that's not the strange part. I'll get to that in a minute.

I took an early train to work. There were many seats available, but a few people opted to stand.

I was by myself on a two-seater in the mostly empty rear of the car, and these two guys were at the nearby set of doors. My CD Walkman's battery died in the middle of an Enya track (I finally found the time to listen to the CD I had bought a few days ago, and then . . .)

I was eavesdropping on the conversation, and it seemed copasetic enough. They were "guys" in that they were talking about some baseball or football game or team. One was older. We'll call him Joe. The other, whose name was Bruce, was closer to my age and had a rather deep voice. I actually know his name because I overheard it while I listened to them.

Joe had this sort of pissed-off look you'd associate with someone who's never been content with what the world has thrown at him: receding hairline before forty, a semi-serious beer belly, day-later shadow on his neck and cheeks, cheap suit worn to cheap-paying job that requires him to wear a suit.

His lips were frowned and motionless like a freeze frame as the younger one expounded upon the merits of the baseball team he favored. "Their line-up this year is the best they've had in my lifetime, and probably yours too," Bruce said with confidence. He cocked his head and grinned.

"I'll give you that, but it's just potential. If they don't live up to it, then the playoffs will be theirs to lose." He arched his eyebrows as he spoke, but Bruce would not accept him as a sage.

"Maybe, but c'mon. It's a dream team. It'll . . ." Bruce continued to speak, but I couldn't hear what he said as the train's wheels screeched as it rounded a bend in the track. The door between the subway cars slid open with the turn, and this amplified the metallic shriek.

It slid closed once the track straightened, and then the train accelerated. The plaintive moaning of the speeding train still muffled the conversation, but Bruce used more gesticulation to amplify his point now. He ground his teeth together, with his mouth open, and then tried to kick Joe. However, the car shimmied and he became unsteady on his feet. Joe's face suddenly turned red with rage, and he hit Bruce hard in the jaw with his free hand. Bruce fell back into the empty seat opposite me. I leapt out of my seat and scurried a few feet away.

The door slid open again. This time a hand with long thin fingers pushed it. A sleekly fitted black laceless shoe peeked through first, and then a thin leg clad in similarly tight black pants. I looked up, and the grinning face that emerged from the darkness was very familiar.

He was the other guy there when I saw the two hillbillies fight in the basement of the music store. As a side note, here's what I wrote about him that day, in short: ***[He] sped down the aisle between the hillbillies and me. He didn't notice the confrontation, or maybe he was just afraid of being around a fight since he walked away fast like a wimp, and mostly stared straight ahead. He turned his head for a split second and winked at me when he passed."*** I barely noticed him that day, but I recognized him immediately this morning. Let's call him Zeke.

Zeke's frame was not quite anorexic thin, but he was a waif. His fine designer apparel and moussed wavy hair indicated a sinister decadence. He was running on empty, but with inhuman ferocity.

He boldly stepped into the subway car and put his bony hands into the pockets of his black jacket. Bruce jumped from the seat and lunged at Joe at this point. Just as Bruce was trying to rip the skin off Joe's shoulder, Zeke slipped beside the scuffling pair, unconcerned by his proximity to the flailing arms and torsos. Zeke was not a frightened bystander. Joe threw Bruce once again with even more force and he landed on the floor. His head slammed into the aluminum door with a hideous cracking noise. A stream of blood steadily spread across the floor from his bleeding scalp. He was unconscious. Zeke continued his sashay by grasping a pole for a dainty spin at the mid-section of the car.

Joe glared at his prostrate buddy as Zeke spun for another loop or two. The rails squealed again, and the people in the sparsely packed car shifted involuntarily in their seats. Zeke spun another loop faster and with more force, but did not stumble. The split second his line of sight passed the fight scene, he mimed a gun with his thumb and forefinger. I looked at Joe, and he had abruptly started crying. His jaw dropped as if released from a vise, and he grabbed some of his remaining hair.

The train now barreled past waiting commuters on the platform of the Lexington Avenue Station. Zeke slowed for one final spin and released his arm in synch with the halting train. He bolted as the doors before him opened.

Joe had slumped down to the floor. He was coddling Bruce. It seemed like Bruce wasn't breathing, and Joe looked inconsolable. "I don't understand what I've done!" he exclaimed. I held out my hand to him, and he shuddered.

The image of Zeke's entrance flashed through my head. When he pushed the door and entered the car, sparks flew from the rails. They illuminated his grinning green eyes for a moment when he stood between the cars. I suddenly realized that every move he made from the moment he entered the car was staged and calculated.

I went back to my description of the fight on Monday and it has only confirmed my theory. He telepathically controlled both fights, per the following text from the other day: ***Roy raised his arm to deliver a blow to the back of Buck's head in a sort of weirdly hesitant slow motion that belied the aggressive anger on his face. His beefy flannel-clad arm was unexpectedly reluctant, but it did its job at the moment of impact with a squishy thud.***

Facial muscles are weaker than arm and leg muscles. That's why the arm was "reluctant." Roy was not completely powerless. Roy fought against Zeke's telepathic effects.

This seems extraordinarily absurd, and the logical side of my mind battled against the idea all day long. I spoke to Constance and Justin about it over a last-minute lunch date I scheduled with them this morning once I got to the office.

Constance is always the voice of reason. After all, she's my only friend who had the guts to go to graduate school. She reads Aristotle all day long.

We ate at the Banyon's Steakhouse in Midtown. I grimly stared at my food while they ate. Then, Justin dangled a chicken tender over his lips.

Constance laughed. "Between you two? Who's more of a challenge?" Justin raised his hand and dropped the fried piece of rotting flesh to the dirty (too dirty for retrieval?) floor. "You shouldn't pretend to be drunk after a single beer with lunch," she said to Justin. "And you?"

"He practically killed the other guy, Constance," I said.

"Can you give them names when you speak about them? All these pronouns are confusing."

She continued to grill me with questions about the mundane elements of the confrontation. Did the police show up? What did they do? Did Bruce survive? There wasn't a single question about Zeke. "What about Zeke?" I finally asked.

"Is he the phantom?" she asked.

"Yes, that's what we'll call him," Justin said, giggling. "He was dancing through the bloodshed. He fiddled whilst Rome burn to the ground!" He paused. "Is Zeke here?" he asked and then goofily looked from side to side.

Constance laughed for a moment but quickly composed herself. She grabbed my hand from across the table and looked me in the eye. "I know that he had nothing to do with those fights. Your observations were just a coincidence. You need to calm down."

May 31, 2003

I had another strange dream last night. It was set in my parents' old house. I was alone in the basement. In the corner of the big green-carpeted basement living room, I was on my computer typing a fifteen-page paper on various economists' perspectives on rent. My computer shared the room with my dad's stereo, Peter's weights and his treadmill.

The assignment page was on the floor, and at the bottom was a bold-faced, underlined, 25-point-font reminder of the expected minimum length. I had old books on my lap and under my chair. Additional ancient tomes sat on the carpet. I had them open to important pages, and I laid them on top of each other to form a pile snaking away from my chair. I stretched to reach down for the book with the James Mill essays toward the back. I didn't tip over on my white plastic chair, but strained my back muscles nonetheless.

I stared at a page in the collection of James Mill essays, but my eyes were . . . The only word I can think of to describe it is paralyzed. This was unusual. While physical paralysis or restriction of movement is a recurrent element in my dreams, my eyes were never paralyzed before. Regardless, I could not summon the energy to move them across the page of the book. I looked up to the screen, but could not get them to read the monitor either. I could look at shapes and see the room, but my eyes would not move across text. In retrospect, I find this strange, but in my dream state, I just figured I was getting bored.

After a few moments the paralysis went away, and I looked at the CDs piled next to the computer. The pile included jewel cases with CDs inside, empty jewel cases, and orphaned CDs who may or may not have belonged to the empty jewel cases. An Enigma CD peaked out from the bottom of the pile. I snagged the disc and pushed the button to open the disc drive, but it didn't open. I pushed it a few more times, and it would not open.

I dropped the CD on the keyboard and plied the rectangular lid open. I arched my index fingers at the sides of the disc carriage and pulled while pushing the small button repeatedly with my thumb. I yanked much harder, and sparks of electricity shot out. The monitor went dark. There was a horrendous hum, and the lights briefly dimmed and then shut off.

I was jolted up from my chair by the electric shock from the disc drive. Smoke and fire simmered from the computer. The room stank from burning plastic. Behind the computer was grandma's old chair with two tall stacks of old magazines on the seat. I shook and spun around in the darkness. My head drooped violently about my shoulders, since I lost control of my neck muscles. I tried to scream, but I was too shocked. I swallowed my tongue as I dropped to the floor. The fire hit the magazines and spread rapidly. It illuminated the room with a husky red glow. Then I woke up screaming.

I sat at my dining table and looked over my apartment. I noticed how clean it was in comparison to my parents' old house. This made me feel safe and I was able to go back to sleep.

June 1

Hunter woke me up at noon with a phone call. She was surprisingly sober and told me about her Saturday night with her white trash friend Sharisse. She said they did "it" and gave each other a "gaggle of orgasms." I complemented her alliteration, and she said she was joking. I knew she was, telling her I wouldn't have cared if they did fuck so long as they invited me to watch.

"Shari is a dyke, you know."

"Isn't that the explanation for Clea? Clea is her . . .?"

"Yeah, but they're bi."

"Cool."

"What's up today?" I explained to her that I had no plans, but was feeling down for no specific reason. It did not behoove me to tell her about the bloody beating or my second death dream within a week. She's grim enough already. She would probably come over for sex to make me feel better, but it would probably make me feel worse because she is so thin now and her bloodshot eyes are more sad than sexy now. I told her about the partial decapitation dream when she called me Thursday afternoon. She didn't say much to console me over the phone, but came over to blow me. When I looked at her freshly frizzled and greasy orange yarn hair and saw her staring up at me with those dark and scary sad eyes, I went limp. She went home, and I reluctantly finished the job. "I can come over," she suggested today, but I refused another round of humiliating consolation head.

Constance and Justin arrived later. He wore a bathing suit and an orange Speedo shirt. Constance looked tired but was smiling. "I'm taking you two to the beach," he said when I opened the door. "You okay, man?" he asked.

"Why?" I shifted to the side to look in the mirror by the door. I hadn't looked at myself in the mirror for days, and I was haggard. I hadn't shaved since Friday morning, and my wavy hair was tangled. My skin looked like moldy white cheese covered in stubble. "I see what you mean. I'm glad you guys showed up."

As I began to prepare a quick but satisfying meal for my friends, I eased back into the Zeke thing. "It's such an enigma. I don't get it."

Constance frowned. "You really need to go to the beach," she said.

"You are making yourself crazy," Justin said and then laughed.

Constance laughed too. "Think about it, Shane. It's so ludicrous."

I guess I needed to go to the beach, so I laughed the topic off with them. Of course, my laugh was more desperate than theirs was. It consisted of panicked breaths and a big fake dimpled smile.

"What are you making, Shane?" Constance asked. She sashayed over to the kitchen to show off her fine, but too conservatively cut hot pink swimsuit. "Yum. Portobello sandwiches with . . . jack cheese on sourdough? California boy!"

"Yeah, I'll probably throw some avocado on 'em too."

Constance likes to make fun of my Cali-philia. I spent my summers there when I was a kid. Mom would drag little Peter and I to the beach. He smoked his first joint out there when he was like ten, I think. I was fifteen, and he was ten. That sounds right. The older kids who provided the pot made a bonfire and he puked on it. I schlepped him back to the hotel. Those were the days!

"It's healthy and light. Great for a day at the beach," I said.

Unfortunately, our plan for a beautiful day was ruined shortly after when the doorbell rang. When I opened the door, a fidgety Hunter and a gum-chewing Sharisse greeted me.

"Who is it?" Constance asked.

I turned around and saw Justin's frown. "Hunter, and . . .?"

Constance walked into the room and stood behind me next to Justin. "Oh God, not Shari too?" Constance whispered to him.

Hunter actually looked better. She had washed her ringlets and was tremulous from withdrawal. I knew it wouldn't last the day, but her effort was almost heart-warming. Sharisse scampered ahead of Hunter and headed straight for Justin. He groaned into his coffee cup. She wore some sort of clingy synthetic shiny body suit (fitted does not suit her and her back fat at all!) and reeked from a liberal application of inexpensive perfume. It smelled like aftershave that one could acquire by the gallon in a ninety-nine–cent store. "Isn't Connie more your speed?" Justin asked, droll as ever.

"I swing both ways, Mr. Simonds." She pulled a chair and sat close to him, invading his personal space. "Especially when one of my choices has got a stick up her ass. That leaves little room for me."

Meanwhile, Hunter slinked past me and parked herself on my couch by the window.

"Hunter?" I called out to her from across the room and then drew closer. I tried to sound sincere and compassionate as I continued. "C'mon, babe." Her face was blank. She sank into the cushions. She wasn't being rude. She was distracted. "That old w/d got you down?"

"Why are they here? That makes it harder for me."

"We're going to the . . .," Justin hollered at Sharisse, but I wasn't paying attention to their conversation on the other side of the living room so I don't know the exact reason for his outburst. I lowered my voice. "We're going to the beach, and your friend is not invited."

She started to sob. "I knew you hated her," she whispered.

"Well, you are making it harder for me now, Hunter. You showed up unannounced with Sharisse, and I have plans."

She covered her eyes with her hand and dropped her head down.

"Don't guilt trip me," I said.

"Admit you hate her," she whispered and withdrew back in the chair.

I pursed my lips and snapped my fingers. "Hey!" She pulled her hand away from her eyes. "I tolerate her because she's your friend," I said sternly. "I am entitled to my right to do so, and that's that."

Sharisse did a little dance on her way to the kitchen and approached Constance, who stood by the door. "You aren't needed in the kitchen, Sharisse," Constance said.

Sharisse turned to Hunter and I. "Cunt!" Sharisse yelled. "Shane's friends aren't nice to me, Hunter!"

Then, Constance escaped to my bedroom and slammed the door.

"C'mon, Shari. You're not . . ."

"Fuck you, Shane. Do I stick my arm up Lamb Chop's ass for a living?"

Justin got the joke and cringed. "Why don't you just leave, Sharisse?" He emphasized the last syllable for far too long. She walked over and slapped him across the head.

He laughed, and she slapped him again. He kept laughing. "What's so funny?"

"She's channeling Zeke, Shane," Justin suggested.

"Chill Justin," I said.

"Who's Zeke?" Sharisse asked.

"Don't ask," Hunter said.

"Please!" Constance hollered from the bedroom. She turned on the television and raised the volume.

Justin sighed. "I'll give this one a try for fun if nobody else is interested." Of course, there were no takers. "Shane saw him within the vicinity of two fights last week, and thinks he telepathically controlled the combatants. He thinks that Zeke is some sort of beast or demon who will contribute to the downfall of civilization."

"Um, with that last part you were putting words in my mouth" Or was he? It was a logical extension of what I had seen. What if there are telepathic individuals programmed to use their power for destruction? That is exactly what Zeke did, especially the second time. Maybe he is a demon, a harbinger of a new form of destruction, a quiet and inconspicuous evil.

"Yikes," Sharisse said once she finished cackling. "Shane is a freak."

I am amazed by how adversaries, like Justin and Sharisse, can form a fleeting camaraderie when they find something they can debunk together.

June 2, 2003

I visited Peter at Mount Sinai today. It was the first time I've seen him since the recent bad turn of his condition, which Aunt Terry described to me in a tense phone call last week.

He sported a wig today. It was for my benefit and consolation, since my hair bias is well known. When someone has full head of colored hair, I can fool myself and believe that the person is younger, or healthier. Of course, he was even more skeletal and pale now, but that wig blunted the shock.

He asked me about the settlement, but gave no advice about investment. "After all, you're trained for that. That's what you did in college," he said. His voice was raspy from the chemo.

"That reminds me. Have you seen Mom and Dad?"

"Not for a while."

"I would think you see more of them these days."

"No. They don't go anywhere. They're still in the same place."

"I'm not surprised by that actually. They are very boring, after all."

He coughed through some weak chuckles. "You still think of them that way?" he asked.

I nodded. "I wish that I could do better, but I can't."

"That doesn't surprise me," he said and laughed weakly again.

"How long has it been?"

"I saw Mom about two weeks ago, and she was different."

"What about Dad?"

"My memory is going now, Shane."

I apologize that I can't write anymore about this encounter. It was too sad.

From the Journal of Constance

October 20, 2002

I met two brothers at the cemetery yesterday. Shane and Peter were burying their dad. I was there to visit Grandma when they caught my attention. They stood over a fresh grave a few yards away. There is no sadder sight than two young men alone at a funeral. I cut short my own mourning, since Grandma died ten years ago and I can return any time.

I needed to console Shane, because he looked so guilty and depressed I thought he was going to jump into the grave and let them bury him alive. His eyes were red from lack of sleep and a frown was sculpted across his face.

I walked toward them. As I drew closer, I noticed that Peter looked very ill. His skin was gray in patches, and he looked nauseous. Shane held his arm around Peter's waist to support his unsteady frame.

The coffin was already in the pit, and their priest had left. "I'm very sorry," I said. Shane looked up from the ground.

"We should leave now. The car has been waiting for over an hour," Shane said to Peter. Peter winked at me. I almost broke down crying right there. "Would you like to join us, ma'am?" Peter asked.

Shane shook his head, without looking at me. "Come now, Peter. I'm sure that she's got better things . . ." He trailed off and stared at me for the briefest moment. "Okay," he said abruptly.

I'm sure Shane said so to make his brother feel better, but I knew that Shane was the one who needed more consolation. Once we were inside the car, the conversation came very easy. Peter started: "I'm glad you showed up, um?"

"Constance."

"I'm Peter, and my grim brother is Shane."

"I don't want to make you uncomfortable, but I should warn you," he said without looking at me, "our Aunt Terry might be uncomfortable when we show up with a stranger."

"Why?"

"She gets paranoid when strangers are in her home." He raised his head to look at me, and I smiled. "She might like you." His frown eased up ever so slightly.

I suspected that their mother had passed also because the family gathered at their aunt's house. When we got there, everyone accosted them.

Peter retreated to a bedroom upstairs to rest once he greeted the myriad of distant relatives. Contrary to Shane's warning, plump and pouty Aunt Terry did not even notice me.

I wound up in the kitchen. I helped another aunt roll up cold cuts for the guests. Aunt Carolina was friendly and verbose. "Somebody must really like turkey," I said, because there was so much turkey and no cheese.

"Their late mother's side was Jewish." I choked up a bit, and she frowned. "Oh, I forgot. You just met the boys. Calvin's beautiful boys, that's what he called them repeatedly during the last few months. He was my brother. Their mother died in March. Two months shy of Shane's graduation. That broke her heart. She always dreamed of that day . . ." She broke down, and I held her hand. "It's such a sad story. I don't know why they brought you here. It's unfair to unload so much tragedy on a stranger."

Carolina took me out to the backyard and explained to me why Shane's parents had died and why Peter himself would soon be gone as well. Their house was in rural Connecticut, and a nearby chemical factory that produced thermometers and other medical supplies had poisoned them due to their "negligence." The factory's disposal of mercury and other toxic poisons had became "inadequate" a few years earlier when a bad winter in 1998 coupled with "negligent" maintenance of certain pipes and tanks below the ground led to "ruptures." These "ruptures" remained unnoticed until it was far too late. More chemicals escaped into the groundwater each year because these unnoticed "ruptures" grew larger and larger.

Shane went away to college the year of that bad winter and only spent one summer at the house. He spent the subsequent summers elsewhere. Thus, Shane's exposure to the chemicals was limited, and he inadvertently evaded the illnesses that plagued his parents and brother because he went away for college. He would have died if he had stayed in that house.

Much later, I found Shane sleeping in the corner of a sofa. I sat beside him until he woke much later on in the evening. I told him that I knew the entire story. "I wouldn't have had the heart to tell you," he said anxiously. "It was Carolina, of course. She told you everything."

"That's her reputation?" I asked.

He nodded. "Did she tell you about the money?"

"No." And neither did Shane.

"Everything," he added a few extra beats to each syllable of the word and spoke softly. He paused and stared in my eyes. "Everything has a price."

I can't imagine how hard it is to be Shane. It's such a grim situation. I gave him my number and told him to call me anytime.

From the Journals of Shane Lasch

June 2, 2003

As expected, Hunter resumed shooting up, and she decided to do so at my place again. When I got home today, my apartment smelled like puke. I knew that I would find her scrunched in the corner of my bathroom or bedroom, bouncy and red-faced. At least she didn't break anything this time.

Her incoherent babbling echoed from the bathroom. "Bingo!" I thought. The puke stench got stronger as I drew closer to the bathroom. "Yes!" She puked in the bathroom this time. That meant easy cleanup.

Unfortunately, this was not to be. The only puke in that bathroom was the pink custard slop that wound up on her shirt and chin. She had puked elsewhere then wandered to the bathroom.

"Where's the puke?" I asked. She grunted. It occurred to me that she consumed my cherry yogurt. This was a clue. "In the kitchen?" I asked. She mumbled some more unintelligible syllables and giggled. "Fucking WHERE?" I yelled.

This was useless. I started looking for the puke in the kitchen and then ran frantically from room to room. Each one stank like rotting milk. "Where's the puke?" I whined to myself repeatedly. I pushed magazines, empty bottles, and junk mail off tables, yanked the cushions off my couch, and pulled the blankets and sheets off my bed. I looked between the mattress and box spring and peered under every bed, table, and chair, except one. Underneath the dining room table was a small, but putrid, and centrally located pile of puke.

(Later)

Hunter is seated at my dining room table, with her arms at her side. She's focused on the cup of coffee that I set out for her about an hour ago. From her perspective, that cup is probably miles away, and it will take enormous effort to reach it. It'll probably take hours. Occasionally one of her drooping arms will flinch or pivot in its socket, but it isn't moving anywhere. I'm sure that she wants it, but if I try to force the now lukewarm beverage down her throat, she'll probably make another mess for me to clean up. She's topless as well. I tossed that vomit-soiled shirt, and if she gives me any crap, I'll remind her of what she did before. With any luck, that will shut her up.

June 3, 2003

When I woke up this morning she was gone and the coffee cup was empty. I hope she put a shirt on before she left.

(Later)

I called Constance to describe the "puke story," and she told me I should reconsider the future of the relationship. "Keep in mind that she'll probably be dead within the year anyway."

"You think?"

She sighed. "I think I'm stating the obvious."

"I agree." With that said, I pulled the plug. It was time to cut my losses.

I did it over the phone, and her response was typical. "I've still got my key, motherfucker!" She slammed the phone and then called back. I answered immediately, and she didn't say a word.

"Was that a threat?" I asked.

"We're going to fuck you up!"

"This is what I'm talking about, Hunter." She hung up and didn't call back.

(Later)

Does Hunter's threat scare me? I thought about this for a while. It's tough, because I don't believe that she's malicious. She'll puke in my apartment, embarrass me in front of my friends, and leave dirty dishes, but this behavior results from her condition. She is not a mean person.

Unfortunately all of my compassion for her is now gone. I truly have none left. Constance hit the nail on the head. Hunter's dead now, and it's all her fault. My role in that nightmare is over.

On the other hand, Zeke is now a fixture in a completely new genre of nightmares. In my dream last night, he walked down a rainy street carrying a tote bag. A bald mugger accosted him on the lonely street and pulled out a knife. Zeke thrust the bag (which was full of coins) into the air and smacked the mugger's arm with a bone-crunching snap!

His limply hanging hand dropped a couple of inches down from the sleeve, revealing more of his wrist. Zeke grinned and his protruding cheekbones glowed in the moonlight. The mugger fell to his knees from shock. There was no blood, just the slightest sound from the tearing of skin. This sound abruptly accelerated before most of that hairy arm slipped out of the sleeve and fell to the ground. It landed with a squishy bounce, just like a rump roast dropped onto a cutting board. The blood dribbled from the arm on the ground and leaked from the remaining stump in his sleeve.

Zeke lunged at the man again. He swung the bag much harder and knocked his head off his shoulders like a golf ball off a tee.

From the Journal of Sharisse

June 3, 2003

Shane is a self-centered creep. Men like Shane make me glad that I'm only a part-time heterosexual, because women don't pull that kind of shit. They have the balls to break up with you face-to-face. Men are cowardly little pigs, and Shane is worse than a rancid dead maggot-filled pig carcass festering in the blistering sun, because he blew her off over the phone!

How nice is Hunter? She didn't even want to tell me about it, because she was afraid that I would team up with my girl Clea and kill the motherfucker. This didn't work, because she was crying on the phone and jabbering about wanting to kill herself. I knew that Shane was responsible for it.

Drugs will fuck a bitch up, but it's second only to what a man like Shane can do. Men can ruin a woman's life more than any other vice. That's for sure. It's a cycle. He treats her bad, and she does more junk. He treats her worse because she does the junk, and then she does more.

The upshot is that my switchblade sister and I are going to be waiting for Shane at his apartment tonight, and we are going to fuck him up!

(Later)

We stood outside of his apartment and waited for him to come home from work. When he got off the elevator and saw us, we definitely intimidated him. Clea may be short and stout, but she looks tough when she spikes her hair. I held a knife by my thigh and glared fiercely.

He stared glumly at the elevator doors as they quickly shut in his face and remained at a distance. He blabbered horseshit about how it was all Hunter's fault. I kicked his apartment door open and he ran away, possibly to the stairs. Clea smiled at me, and I laughed. "Wanna bet how long it takes for him to get the balls to return to his own apartment?"

"He's going to feel the fear, babe. Feel the fear."

"Hell fucking yeah!"

I'm not sure if we've gotten our full pound of flesh, but this'll do for now. After all, Shane is one paranoid motherfucker. The Zeke thing is a good example.

From the Journals of Shane Lasch

June 5, 2003

I pulled open the curtains in my bedroom last night before I went to sleep, because I wanted the bright Saturday morning sun to wake me up. The red-orange grapefruit sun drew me from my slumber very early. I opened the window, and the crisp wind of the unseasonably cool morning massaged my shoulders. I walked around my apartment for a while wearing just my pajama bottoms.

Then I dressed in my blue running outfit and dark sunglasses. I headed for the park that's just a few blocks from my building.

I marked a start line in the tar-colored gravel of the quarter mile track and started ferociously. The muscles in my legs tingled as if they were just waking up. After a few minutes, my blood boiled as it pulsed through my veins. Another driving pulse, the frenetic electronic music playing in my headphones, facilitated this drive. A fierce momentum drove me forward, and after a mile and a half, I got my jogger's high. Once I had enjoyed three laps of this blissful energy, I was in the second lap of my third mile.

Afterward I rang Justin from a pay phone, and we arranged to meet for breakfast at the donut shop. My energy and enthusiasm surprised him. "Did you stay in last night?" he asked over the phone.

"Yes," I responded.

"Hunter usually drags you out on Friday nights. Right?"

"Not every week. We broke up actually. I'll tell you about it over donuts," I said, now slightly grim.

Justin takes forever to get out of bed on weekends, so I had another hour and a half. I went for another run and aimed to get my runner's high back. A bit later, my neighbor Sandra arrived on the track. She . . . Here comes Justin. I'll resume this later.

(Not much later)

Justin has the attention span of a toddler. In the time it took him to swallow two jelly-filled donuts, I told him the "puke story" and explained how it was the impetus for the breakup. "She's hot. It's a shame, but I won't miss her bitch friends," he said.

"Yeah, but it's going to make my life better."

He laughed and got another donut. "Anything new with that guy who starts the fights? Zeke?" he asked before he began to ingest.

"No." What's the use? As if he would believe any of it! It'd just be entertainment. It would answer the $64,000 question: how crazy is Shane now?

When we emerged from the donut shop, he asked me if I was game for a party later. I told him I would give him a call as we separated. I then ducked into the nearest Sterling Subs and puked up my donuts in the bathroom.

June 6, 2003

I called Constance to tell her about how I dumped Hunter. She was happy to hear that I had the guts to do it. She nagged me to go with her to an art gallery uptown this afternoon. I said "sure" and went to my apartment to take a shower.

(Much later)

The exhibit at the gallery featured watercolor paintings of starving foreign children. The artist is the foremost one to emerge not only from that impoverished nation, but the entire continent as well. (Was it Africa, South America, or Asia? I really can't remember.) They played a really annoying CD with authentic indigenous music by performers who had actually suffered from diphtheria and dysentery. Constance bobbed her head sympathetically, in accord with the other overdressed constipated student loan deadbeats.

I tried very hard to join them. I read about the diseases I couldn't pronounce. I gasped at the crude depiction of sores on the figures' skin, and tumors emerging from the limbs of stick figures that sardonically depicted the extreme starvation that ravaged the population.

One of Constance's friends, who only wore hemp and whose overgrown hair was woven like a hemp garment, spit out facts and figures that would make you want to kill yourself. "In the first ten years of their lives, less food is made available to them than you eat in one month. . . . The average life expectancy is twenty-six. I'm twenty-five. If I lived there, within the year I would be dead." His name was Chuck.

The very healthy-looking artist, who had graduated from Cooper Union, emerged wearing a designer suit. He stood behind a podium at the front of the room as everyone began to clap. He shook his head. "Please. Please. Please." Someone whistled.

"They call me an artist, but I'm not." The room exploded with applause. "They can hear you. Whether they're still on Earth or not, they can hear you." Everyone clapped hard and many cheered as the artist preened. Then, I screamed as loud as I could, but couldn't hear myself over all the applause and cheering. Constance patted me on the shoulder.

Afterward, we went for coffee. Chuck dominated the conversation with further details. "Katami's [the artist] work is less condescending than that of others coming from the region now. He's not trying to impress us with his command of intricate composition. It's pared down work."

"He isn't hiding his message," I suggested. "It's raw."

"Of course," he said patronizingly. "By excising the detail, he starkly reveals what's ineffable to the Western audience. It is a barren and hopeless landscape. We will and should continue to offer economic support, but their plight will always be hopeless."

"That's very existential," I said.

"Yes, it is." He sighed. "As I was saying before . . ." I made a few more comments, and he continued to give me terse and uninterested responses.

From the Journal of Chuck

June 7, 2003

The exhibit was fair. I can think of better ways to spend a Saturday afternoon. It was silly, because Katami, the Cambodian artist who specializes in crude charcoal drawings of skeletal children, was so humble that it became condescending. In addition, he did not use the watercolors effectively. His palette of citrus colors with black and gray was crass and incongruent with his subject. In short, he should stick to the charcoal. Regardless, I cheered along with all the others, because I didn't want to seem like a dick.

Constance brought a slightly menacing preppie she knows named Shane. He interrupted the flow of the group's conversation all day long with banal comments, which indicated he must have went to a no-name university and majored in something less precise and technical than sociology.

I do have to give him credit, since his madness livened things up shortly before we disbanded. He rambled about this guy named Zeke, who he believes is the harbinger of the next apocalypse. Along with others like him, he telepathically manipulates others to battle to the death. I cannot believe that I wrote the last two sentences.

Shane's a raving loon, and I put him in his place quite nicely. "Your hubris is incredible. Do you actually believe that this destroyer would announce himself and his kind to you alone before anyone else?" I asked. He stuttered, trying to respond, but went silent. "It's absurd!"

I was going to rant and rave some more, but it was useless. Once he composed himself, he continued to defend his observation. "I saw it. It was a slaughter."

"I would have read about it in the newspaper for sure," Sasha, sensible as ever, added.

"Exactly," I said.

"Below the radar. The . . ."

She interrupted. "Do you expect us to believe that the dozens of people in that subway car sat idly by while one man beat another to death with his bare hands?"

"Exactly! That's why your story is implausible. Somebody would have done something to break them up," I said huskily.

"It's . . ." He gesticulated violently and raised his voice. Constance put down her espresso and tried to hold him back. "A new evil. People like him. It could all end."

"I'm leaving," Sasha said. "Wanna come with me?" she asked. I nodded, and she immediately left.

On my way out, while Sasha waited outside, Constance promised me that she would take him home and make sure that he was all right. I nodded and pushed past her because I didn't really care.

My evening went uphill from there. Sasha took me to a boring party in a Soho loft full of skanks, and once Sasha had a few, she wanted to go to her place across the street for "real fun" with one of her friends and I.

Who knew Sasha had a friend who's so . . . skilled? I fucked Sasha until she faked her orgasm most convincingly, and then her friend blew me. I'll spare you all the rocket ship and ejaculation metaphors, and go the vacuum power route instead; that girl could suck a volleyball out of garden hose. If I ever choke on an olive, she's the girl to call. Wow!

From the Journals of Shane Lasch

June 9, 2003

I saw Zeke again today, but now know his name is really Jed. I didn't see him on the train this time. My third encounter with the beast was very different.

I decided to snag an iced soy latte after lunch at Club Cafe. I did not notice him in the store while I waited on line because I had fixed my eyes on the pound cake slices in the pastry display case the entire time.

Once I had procured my beverage and reached the condiment island, I sensed evil. I didn't see him yet, but my heart beat faster. I shook a hefty dose of cinnamon into my coffee with my tremulous hand.

Then, out of the corner of my eye, I saw him seated by the window with another guy. We'll call him Diesel, because I didn't catch his name and it's the most appropriate nomenclature. I'm sure that he wears more than his share of those gay-boy jeans. Today, he had paired them with a shiny and skimpy shirt that gave the impression that he was about to go to the local gay disco for chorizo. This isn't surprising, because Jed always struck me as a straight-acting fag. They might be a couple.

Jed stood up, and the chair leg scratched across the gray tiles. He mumbled a profanity or two, but grinned sinisterly. He grabbed his drink and walked toward me. His wan drawn cheeks, which emphasized his angular jawbone, frightened me.

I looked around the store at the others and feared that I would be next. The patrons were mostly middle-aged middle managers from the surrounding skyscrapers. Nobody was conspicuous, except me. It would have been very plausible to any random onlooker that I was more likely to start a fight than anyone else in that place beside Jed and his buddy. I realized that I could die right there, or worse, that I would lose my free will and beat someone to death with my own hands. The headline on the cover of the ***Post*** for June 7, 2003, would read: "Death by Coffee." "Which Club Cafe?" Manhattanites everywhere would collectively ask over their double espressos.

I nervously shook more cinnamon into my drink. I tried to stop when I realized my drink would no longer be edible if I were to continue. He remarked, "Dang!" with no discernible southern accent when he reached the stand. Dang? Was that an allusion to the encounter in the music store?

I dropped the cinnamon shaker down hard. It sprayed up a cloud of spice, and I sneezed. "You really like that shit," he said. He grabbed some packets of artificial sweetener and tore one open. He cackled, "Sugar shot" and poured the contents down his throat. "Coffee with aspartame. Heh. I've skipped lunch."

Is he a vampire? Vampires don't eat, right? I thought. I took a swig to see just how spicy I had made my coffee.

"Jed Hell," he said.

I choked. My tongue was numb from the excess cinnamon. Grainy coffee leaked from my mouth.

"It's just a name," he said.

"Hell, as in?"

"Oh, I'm sorry. Its spelled H-A-E-L-E. I can see how you would think . . ."

"I'd pronounce it 'hale'."

"That's right. That's what I said."

"No. You said 'Hell.'"

"I don't recall. So many pronunciations, so little time." He shook his head. "Watch the spice, man. You know you'll puke if you have too much." I did not know that. He turned away and returned to his friend. He didn't say anything. They just laughed. Apparently, Jed's tactic for today was old-fashioned ragging. I wasn't going to be goaded into a fight by him. I held my head high and headed for the exit. It's unwise to fight when the odds are unquestionably stacked against you!

Of course, this presupposes that you possess your free will. I did not.

My legs froze in place once I reached the door. I grabbed for the door handle, but released because my legs were stuck in place as if they were made of concrete. Diesel pointed toward me, and Jed turned his head and glared.

The rest of my body went numb, and the coffee cup fell from my limply hanging hand. However, I did not fall. He must have held me up telepathically. I felt like I was levitating, but the floor was still five feet and nine inches below my line of sight. My eyes were the only body part that I could move and control.

Jed's smooth voice and his friend's horn-like laughter overpowered all other background noises. "And then he stopped shaking it . . ."

An impatient middle-aged middle manager pushed my arm aside on his way out. It swung up across my chest and face and fell back down. My unmoving bulk still blocked his way. Diesel let out another hearty yelp. Jed winked and the suit grabbed my shoulder. He pushed much harder this time, but released again. When he gave up, all my sensation returned. I quickly shifted out of the way.

My leg was wet and cold. I had splattered sooty coffee on my tan khakis. I wiped my nose. It was bleeding.

"Rusty pipes?" Diesel asked.

"Are you all right?" someone else asked.

I nodded to no one in particular. "It's just a nose bleed." I hope! I think if I had a stroke, I wouldn't be able to do all this writing.

The encounter disoriented me so much that I sat down on the closest chair. It was by the floor-to-ceiling window, a few seats away from them. Jed returned to his coffee. He took a swig and sucked in his already hollow cheeks. He put the cup down and folded his long fingers together.

Then something weird happened. I lost control of my eyes. They pivoted from the dimmed light above me to the spreading puddle of coffee at my feet. They turned to the employee with a mop on one side to Jed and Diesel on the other. I tried to resist by facing front, but my eyes fixed on the following people for a split second on the street outside: a transient in a hurry, a tall butch female executive smoking the longest cigarette I ever saw, a female model dressed incognito with sunglasses and silky tan hair hanging out of a pea cap, and a guy with model quality features and poise showing off his physique in a muscle shirt and fitted black jeans. My eye followed him and fixed on his toned ass, which must be perfect or else Jed wouldn't have forced my eyes to focus on it.

Just like before, Jed abruptly halted his control. At this point, I realized that he was only toying with me and that physical danger was not a concern for today. Rather, I inferred that he wanted to communicate. "So, Jed. I saw you at a music store about two weeks ago," I said.

"Which one?" Jed asked.

"The one off Eighth Avenue and 42nd Street."

Jed grinned at me, and Diesel laughed. "That store closed six months ago," Diesel said.

"Yeah, man. You're right," Jed said to Diesel. "You're wrong."

This is a new conundrum, because I am wrong. That store did go out of business six months ago.

I have a theory. It has to do with my memory. The record store closed long before May 26, 2003, and the food court where I claimed to have eaten in this journal closed months ago as well. The solitary trip to the city I described for the afternoon of May 26, 2003, could not have happened on that day. The excursion really happened sometime in the past. I remember it. There was a fight between two hicks, but it wasn't two weeks ago. It was last year. The more I think about it, the more that I realize that I was writing about a memory from the past on May 26. Those events happened last summer, when I was out of school and going on interviews. Most of my interviews were in the morning, and I spent many afternoons at that food court and record store. I can't pinpoint the exact day, but I now know two things: I first saw Jed sometime last summer at the record store, and he has sporadically controlled my mind and body for some time now. He used his powers to incite violence in others, briefly paralyzed me today, and manipulated my perception of time for an extended period of time.

Jed's powers are vile, and I now wonder if he is the only one. What if he is part of an emerging breed of individuals with this power? They can control the actions and thoughts of others. What else can they do? These people are an insidious threat because they don't reveal themselves. I saw one man die. Who knows how many others have died, with no media coverage or public awareness. They can destroy civilization gradually, and nobody will be able to identify the threat. Their "gift" is a legitimate threat.

June 10, 2003

Aunt Terry rang me this morning at five to tell me that Peter has like no time left. I shuddered in my room for what felt like hours, but by the time I left, it was only a few minutes past six.

When Mom died last March, Dad and I went to the funeral thinking that Peter would go next. He wasn't well enough to leave the house. It was too cold.

Dad told me about when Mom gave birth to him. Peter was premature by a few weeks. He was healthy, but small. Dad was in the delivery room for his birth to make up for when he chickened out when I was born. Mom had them play new-age music. The music was flowing and gentle, and that

Peter transcended all the grit and mess of childbirth. He was a bloody angel, with aqua eyes and a button nose.

Dad said he never loved Mom more than he did at that moment, not when she was dying and not on the day that he married her. "It is the moment I will remember when I die," he said when we stood over her grave. I wish that I could have been part of Peter's birth, but I was five and had stayed at home with Aunt Carolina. She had made me blueberry pancakes every day.

When they brought Peter home, it was a hot summer day. Mom ached all over. Dad was exhausted and slept for two days. There was precious little magic, and I hated the little bastard because of all the attention he received.

Dad reminded me of this also when we buried Mom. I had forgotten about it for years. A repressed memory emerged; when eleven-month-old Peter said "water," I went to slap him. Mom stopped me. I wanted him to go away.

This flood of memory augmented my guilt on that obnoxiously sunny spring afternoon when we buried Mom. I wanted to un-wish the wishes I made when I was five a million times. "Peter's next," I said softly, as I stared down into the grave.

This was not to be. Dad died next, of course. He was diabetic to start with, and that didn't help. Of course, Dad's death was the turning point, because I met Constance, and through our friendship, I broke away from much of this misery. My family encouraged this friendship for my mental well-being, as I grew grimmer with each trauma.

The oncology wing hallway smelled like death yet again this morning. That familiar putrid mold smell is always pervasive. It attacked me once the elevator doors parted, along with the usual somber hum of soft-speaking nurses and the dementedly bright florescent white light.

His room was a long walk from the elevator. I walked toward it slowly, and my pace rapidly slacked. I was still far from his room, but I could not go on. I just couldn't.

I tried to console myself for being such a coward. ***Maybe he's comatose now,*** I thought.

No! He died conscious. He had last words, and then he died. Carolina called me later on to advise me of this, and I finally understood that her amicability is the sleaziest disguise. "You should have been there," was the first thing she said. Her tone was icy. "I'm okay with this," was the second thing she said; these were Peter's last words. He said them in reference to me not being there. She repeated those four words a few times with more rage each time. "How dare you!" she finally yelled. "Your father would have disowned you if he were still alive!"

"I'm sure that this is all about Peter! Right?"

"How dare you! How dare you insinuate . . ."

I cut that bitch right the fuck off. "How dare I? How dare I get all the money! Yes, the settlement! It's all mine, and your guilt trip mind fucks won't work on me. You still have your family, Carolina, so fuck you!"

No, I did not hear Peter's last words. I did not watch the last member of my family fade away. I've done that twice so far and could not do it again.

I thought I was going to hurl from the stench of death in that cancer ward when I paused in that hall this morning. It's like body odor, unrelenting and stagnant. It's like burnt rancid meat. Everybody on that floor was rotting toward the grave.

The pudgy nurse smiled. "It's all right," she said. I shook my head at her. She frowned and swiveled around in her chair. Then, I ran away.

I cried in the elevator, but once I got to the street, my feelings intensified. I sat down on an empty bench and my somber tears turned into retching. I couldn't breathe. I did not have the wherewithal to return, and nobody has the right to judge me for that.

June 11, 2003

Carly took it better than my landlady did. Carly sighed. "Thanks for the two weeks' notice." On my way out of her office, which has a view of Times Square, she chirped, "Hope you enjoy California, buddy."

My landlady was less amused. Fern snarled at me in her Eastern European accent. "You prayed to my shit to get the apartment, and now you blow me off with no notice. FUCK YOU!" She used to bring me her leftover meatloaf on Sunday afternoons. Who would have thought?

I have wanted to move to San Diego for years, and now I will. It's seventy degrees plus or minus ten 98 percent of the year, with almost no rain. La Jolla is the place to be if you are young and wealthy. I'm joining the ranks of the nouveau riche. I'll buy a huge wardrobe of designer clothes at the mall. If I want to snag the right apartment and fit in, then my current drab wardrobe will not work, no matter how much money I have.

June 12, 2003

The funeral was today. Peter's skin looked healthier than the last time I saw him. That still creeps me out big time at funerals.

I drank a lot afterward. I slept for a while and dreamt of hurling into the casket. Instead, I hurled over Aunt Terry's leather sofa. Her chatty twin twelve-year-old daughters glared at me from recliners by the window. That was nothing new. Everybody glared at me today.

On my way out the front door of my aunt's house for the last time, I heard her scream. I slipped on my headphones and walked across her lawn. I stepped on a few of her flowers. The fiery light of the setting sun bathed it with an eerie orange glow. I grinned all the way to the train station. It was all done.

June 13

Ten reasons why I will not write a journal anymore:

1) All the problems that motivated me to write, except one, are all gone.
2) I'm moving to the happiest place on earth after Disneyland. And as it turns out, San Diego is just a hundred miles south of it.
10) Forty million dollars.

I can skip to ten, because I don't have to answer to anyone any more ever again.

June 14, 2003

I saw Diesel, whose name is really Dean, at the mall in Midtown while I shopped for a bathing suit. I had chosen my items, and when I headed for the register, I noticed him. Dean was comically cruising the swimsuit-clad male mannequins right by the register. I didn't want to look around for Jed, but I knew he was there. Dean pointed to the mannequin's torso. "You should try it on for size," he remarked to me. I don't think he recognized me from before.

"I'm sure you'd love to see that," I said. I held up my more conservative low-cut trunks. He arched his head swiftly and turned to walk away.

Then, Jed speed walked past me. His wayfarers bobbed from a chain across his chest. He grabbed Dean. "Dean! We need to go to this new bar called Maran now. The cologne sprayer guy upstairs swears by it."

They were gone so quickly that I couldn't help but wonder if Jed, in all his omnipotent power, did not notice me. He had inadvertently provided me the opportunity to accost him in a situation where he's vulnerable. I took my time and intended to give him an hour to liquor up while I finished shopping. It took me an extra half hour to find Maran, so I arrived almost two hours later. It was a disappointing sight. Dark grime caked the floor, and the wooden bar was lightly tanned from overwashing. It shined weakly in the dim orangey light. The small tables were haphazardly spread about the floor. There were bookcases against the walls with old books and other dusty artifacts. This was not a new place, but it drew a decent late-afternoon crowd that grew while I was there. However, the bar, where Dean and Jed sat, remained sparsely occupied.

They sat toward the middle of the bar, nursing low-carb beers. I sat at the end by the door and ordered "what they're having" from the spunky female bartender. Dean looked at me. "Buddy," he said. Jed smiled weakly and, as if to toast me, held up his bottle. I felt oddly serene and comfortable. I didn't have heart palpitations or any anxiety.

For a while, they chatted and ignored me. I drank vodka shots. When I overheard that they were switching to vodka, I shifted over two seats. "You guys can make it a double if you want. I'm buying."

The bartender poured their singles first and Jed stared at the small glass. "High-proof booze has the least carbs. Did you guys know that?" I asked.

Dean nodded his head. "Of course," he said. "We'll definitely take you up on that offer," he said to me.

Jed agreed. The hocked it back. I leaned down and strained to grab my bag from the end of the bar and nestled it in my lap. "You went shopping today?" Jed asked.

"I'm moving to California next week," I said and then downed my shot. I am sure that Jed has better things to do than find a single person in a state as large as California.

"You need summer clothes there," Jed remarked.

"All year 'round," Dean added. "You'd need them if you stayed here too. Summer's coming."

Jed grinned. "Yeah. It gets hot and loud, and people get into fights on the streets. It's a fucking riot."

"A riot?" I asked. Something, somewhere in my head pulsed.

"Oh. Thank you, ma'am," Jed said to the bartender after she poured the double shots. Jed slipped it down without any grimace at all. "I love your hair," he said to her.

"A riot?" I asked again.

"Yeah, bub. More so every year, it seems."

My brain pulsed harder, and my lower right eye-lid twitched. "Do you feel remorse?" I asked.

"Why should I?" He asked curtly

"Why should he?" Dean added.

"It's just . . . an observation." They sighed, and I left the bar. I was now satisfied.

I spoke a little too soon yesterday. The "exception" no longer vexes me, because I realize that I am running away from it. Thus, all the problems that motivated me to write will be gone when I get on that plane.

Part 2
The Writer

From the Literary Exercises/Journal of Jed Haele

June 14, 2003

Sorry for the gap. I've been busy revising that untitled novel that went nowhere about the dope fiend with a heart of gold and all the people who loathe him in spite of his amicability who gets clean and becomes a patronizing holier-than-thou creep. I'm getting repetitive as a writer, and it's boring. My journalizing has yielded diminishing returns lately. Thus, a month-long gap since the last entry.

Fortunately, the worm has turned. I had a fascinating and disturbing encounter today that tied into a mundane incident earlier this week.

Dean and I were at Club Cafe after lunch on Monday. This creepy guy with mischievous eyes and a slight limp leered at us and sat nearby. His name was Shane.

Before he sat down, he paused by the exit and pondered as if he couldn't decide whether he wanted to stay or go. A suit knocked into him, and he spilled his coffee all over. Then the fucker freaked out. He shook and shuddered, and blood dripped from his nose.

He finally sat down near us and tried to make conversation, but it didn't make any sense. He claimed to have met me recently at a music store that closed months ago. Then, he mumbled something about a fight on the E train that ended in death. I think that I would have read about that in the newspaper. I set him straight on both issues, and he abruptly bolted from the store.

I saw him again today at the mall shopping for swimwear. Shane was lanky and clad entirely in black except for a horizontal white stripe on his shirt. Coincidentally I was shopping with Dean again today, as gay guys know their way around fitted summer clothes. We separated for a bit, and when I found him, he was conversing with Shane. I pulled him away, because you can't be too careful. Shane could be gay, but he seemed more like a perpetual closet case. Such a person would not take a flamer's advances in the middle of a well-lit and crowded store very well.

I dragged Dean away, we went to a bar, and wouldn't you believe it, the freak followed us there. He loitered outside for a few minutes and then came in, sitting near Dean and me at the bar. He bought us vodka shots and offered to make them doubles. I must have smirked. Was this guy for real?

Then, he went ape shit over something I said and made a bunch of accusations. "It's just that you're responsible for all those injuries and deaths." He paused. Dean turned to me and scrunched his face. I mimicked the expression to Shane. "Don't you look at me like that!" Shane growled, louder.

"Like what?" I asked.

"Like that," Dean suggested to Shane. "It's the only reasonable way to respond. You just called my friend a murderer."

Shane bopped his head around in many directions. I thought he was going to get whiplash. "It's only appropriate," he continued louder. "It's only appropriate! Because it's true!" He tapped his right fist on the bar.

"Huh?" I asked.

"Huh?!" Shane mimicked. "This is more than an observation, Jed! I experienced it myself. I experienced your power! Your gruesome . . ." Dean laughed, and Shane snarled at him. "You are a beast, as well."

I was perplexed. "Calm down, man. Just explain it to me. What do you think I did?" He banged his right fist on the bar. "No. Don't do that. Talk to me!" I pleaded, and he spit on my shirt. He grabbed his bag and bolted for the door.

"Stop!" I yelled.

He stopped and turned around. "My own free will. I stop by my own free will," he said grimly. "You would take away my free will. That's what he can do, people!" he yelled. "That's what he can do!" More people noticed him now, and a few laughed.

"That's . . . ridiculous. Absolutely ridiculous," the bartender said. Shane shook his head and returned to the bar. Dean guzzled both of our double vodka shots in an instant and let out a big cackle. I reached out for Shane's hand, and his furious visage abruptly turned into a blank stare.

Shane banged his hand on the bar much harder and broke the skin on two of his knuckles. The sound was louder than the music. "He's a beast!" He slammed his reddening fist again, and the anger returned to his face. My empty shot glass shook. All the patrons laughed now. Some of the guys hollered.

"He can control your minds!" He banged it again. The shot glass popped up a few millimeters off the bar and fell back down. "He can kill you all with his mind!" His knuckles dripped blood, and he rapped the hand on the grimy wood bar with full force once more. My glass bounced off the bar and shattered into bits on the floor. The bones under the skin squished as he propped it up with his other hand. The roaring of the patrons turned to hushed and amazed whispers. I was in shock. I couldn't move.

He turned white and continued weakly. "It will all end, because of people like them." He allowed his bludgeoned hand to drop by his side, placed the other one to his cheek, and sobbed. Someone shut the music off. "We should call a doctor," one person said. "I'll call 911," another person yelled. One final slam interrupted all of these muffled comments.

With every bit of power and force he could muster, Shane yelled, "DESTROYER!" and fully shattered his hand against the bar.

He propped the mangled flesh up to his face with the other hand. It no longer resembled a hand. The digits were intact, but the knuckles had separated and the skin between them tore as they descended. A fresh stream of blood squirted from the skin that split to shreds between his knuckles and flowed down his wrist.

He pulled the other hand away, and the shattered piece of flesh flopped down onto his face limply. He dropped to his knees. "I don't mean to sound callous, Jed, but . . ." Dean paused. The unexpectedly limber bartender jumped over the bar to calm the crowd. ". . . but he's a writer's dream."

There was nothing left to do except to jot my e-mail on a napkin and slip it in Shane's pocket on the way out. Surely this "writer's dream" won't hesitate to use it when he recovers. You can type with one hand, right?

June 15, 2003

I don't expect to get an e-mail from Shane for a few days at least, so I have to let that drop for now.

Pardon the cliché, but the natives are getting restless. How did my second job get so consuming? There's profit, but there's also pressure. They are so desperate for that vicarious thrill. They don't pick it up when I mock "them." "Them?" I met three of "them" at a college party once. I was discussing the prospects for mainstream marketing of ***Dance of the Damned*** with Janine, when three jerks bopped over. "You the man!" one of them said.

Ugh. I smiled. "In the flesh, Jed Haele," I said cordially.

"We pronounce it HELLLLLL!" one of the others yelled, followed by a ***long*** beer burp.

"You would. Nice meeting you guys. Keep reading. The next one will be . . ." I paused and nodded. "You'll like it." That was a Christmas or end of the semester party, I think. Why do I allow Janine to drag me to college parties? I can't wait until she graduates, because it's embarrassing. Many of my readers go to her school, and I know that she communicates with them. I'd be very embarrassed if they found out that I allow my typist so much latitude. Unfortunately, I am not close enough with her to ensure that she is discreet about such things.

Her suggestions are always excellent. My original title for ***Dance of the Damned*** was ***Last Things You'd Expect***, because it's a book about the last things you'd expect a preppie to do, like having a sex change, murder, hustling, and not paying retail. Janine argued that since he's terminally ill, understands that his actions are evil, and his encounter with God is imminent, his actions are a dance by a damned man. I reminded her that I was an atheist, but could not argue with the fact that her title fit the text far better.

Then again, I should be careful what I wish for, because she may not be willing to type and make "editorial revisions" for five dollars a page once she graduates next year. I can just imagine the scene. She will have let herself into my apartment with her extensions flopping about, fresh from her commencement, carrying a velvety red diploma case, plunking it down on my lap. She'll stand there with her arms crossed staring at me sternly without saying a word. I'll stumble out some syllables, and she will begin effusively. "I got a degree now, and a job. I can still do your job, but we're talking about my downtime now. I get paid overtime when working through my downtime." She goes on and on until I give her a 50 percent raise. That'd be $1,400 for a 280-page book.

Of course, that wouldn't fuck up my profits too much, as I do quite well. The last time I checked, I have 1,913 subscribers who pay thirty each for a novel:

1,913
x 30
$57,390

Thus, her raise would not make much of a dent in my profits. It's not bad for six months of work, plus a few shorts thrown in here and there.

That's what Shane will be. I'll write a nice short, or possibly a novella. It depends on how crazy he is. We'll see.

(Later)

Could Shane be a novel? It's not that I want to write a novel about Shane, but it's been nine months since ***Dance of the Damned***. It will take me at least that long to fix ***Untitled***. Maybe longer?

The two periods of Gabriel's life that I depict in ***Untitled*** are the "junkie with the heart of gold" and the later "sanctimonious chain-smoking bible thumper." The book was supposed to be about these nifty transitions between past and present. They were supposed to show that any past, even one clouded by addiction, will make the present appear cheap and disappointing in comparison.

In addition, I wanted the transitions to weave into abstract fiction for some stretches of the novel. Unfortunately, the transitions just don't work! I read my handwritten draft last night and stopped on page twenty-nine when I started doing the rapid cuts between the two periods. They are obvious, pointless, and confusing. For instance:

I preach to the wicked on the subway after work at least twice a week, before they go off to indulge, and have sticky encounters in bars and clubs. I feel sorry when I look at those sculpted pretty faces. They don't know what they do, but that does not affect the Lord's will. Not one bit!

If I had overdosed one of those damned nights, he would have cast me away to hell, and I would have deserved it. The righteous only deserve his mercy. Demons will burn. The bright fiery light of hell will engulf them.

The sun was like an atomic bomb. It woke me up today, when Sally lifted the garage door. I yawned and cracked my ankles. She popped into the Le Sabre. I reached into my pocket and put on my Wayfarers.

She slammed the door and opened the window. "Close the fucking garage door after I pull out, babe," she chirped bitterly. I tried to go to the office today, but could not pry myself off the cold hard floor of my garage for hours.

I made it until the early afternoon. The body gets what it wants, one way or another.

I met my dealer outside the shopping center. He cut me a good deal for some reason and introduced me to his "friend."

Untitled is the same old downward spiral, interspersed with the ranting and raving of a wannabe preacher. "Haele's most grim and patronizing one yet," would be the review quote inside the paperback's cover, if the book were actually published.

Per the excerpt, the crosscutting device is lame and the message gets too obvious. It's a disaster. I think that I have to split the past and present into two distinct halves, with the entire text of one following the other. This sort of revision is like splitting that atom for the first time from scratch without the benefit of twentieth century physics.

Thus, Shane's story could be my easy out, but it may not be meaty enough to fill a novel. I'm going to discuss him with Janine over drinks tomorrow. I'll bounce my ideas off her.

June 16

I met Janine at Maran, which is the bar where Shane mutilated himself at on Saturday afternoon. The same bartender was there. It wasn't busy, so I asked her to describe it to Janine. She obliged, I gave her a twenty-dollar tip, and then we moved to a table.

"What was the point of that?" Janine asked, perplexed. "He's a mental case. That's your rut. You only write about fucked-up losers."

"I know, but this guy is different and I can bridge different themes and genres like never before: thriller, apocalyptic science fiction, coming of age, and confused sexuality, because you just know that he wrote me off as a fag along with Dean. There is a story, but my novel twist is that there will be redemption. He'll destroy himself, and somehow that will set him free. That's what I tried to do with, um . . ."

She smirked. "***Untitled.***"

"The mess," I added. ***Jesus. I should start paying you a retaining fee or something***, I thought, but didn't say. "I think I can bang out ***Shane*** real fast," I said.

"Is that official?" She asked slyly

"It's a working title," I said. We both chuckled. "What do you think? It will be a sublime finale to the first three."

"A trilogy with a redemptive finale, and a new breed of nut-job." She thought hard. She scrunched her brow. Her forehead wrinkles when she does this. "Maybe," she said distractedly, and finished her drink.

"Maybe?"

She sighed hard. "Maybe ***Shane*** could be a short story or novella. That would buy you time, so you could fix ***Untitled.***" She bobbed her head rhythmically with the light dance music. "It would be so enigmatic. You could take the hand scene and surround it with little or no contextual details or storyline. That would fuck with them real good. It could be an excellent short piece. I think it would get too diluted if you tried to pull a novel out of it."

I shook my head. "I think that I can build a novel out of this if I am resourceful and interact with him again."

"Watch out for yourself," she said.

"I will."

"Okay. Got to go, man. Call me. I'll be home weeknights this month."

I finished my drink alone and grew more anxious.

June 17

My subscribers might abandon me if this break goes on too long. I haven't gotten any new ones since April. I'm glad this isn't my only income, but I still wish it were more. I wish that the quality and expectations were elevated. I write commercial trash with a gory and weird edge that you can't get in the bookstores. I can do better than that.

I went to the gym this afternoon and ran five miles on the treadmill. I thought about my options while I worked out. My only idea was to turn ***Untitled*** into a short story (hack it to bits!) or a novella (do less pruning!). I have to be able to pull something out of three hundred and fifty pages.

June 18

I got in touch with my writing buddies this week and met with them at Maran tonight. Dean tags along when we get together, because he usually has nothing better to do. Ever since that low-rated reality show, he has been unemployed and has lived off his winnings. Dean is not a writer. I have three writing buddies.

Makiko and Beatrice are the lesbian couple who work together and separately. They co-wrote two books of poetry that a small local press called Truffle published. In addition, Makiko wrote a terrible novel about lesbians and drugs many years ago. She doesn't even bother to defend it.

Yost is the only one who's still in college. He has the least experience, but I respect his opinion most. His name is fake, and I never pressed him for the real one. It's an acronym that stands for "Your Own Story Teller," i.e., an author. He hates all my novels and has spent the better part of a year on a single chapter of his own novel. He's read more books than any other person in the group has and has an excellent memory. Thus, he can always name a novelist who has handled the subjects that I've chosen first and better. He is not fucking around.

Yost arrived first and began with more criticism. "That thing you are working on is awful. I don't want you to have Janine e-mail any more chapters. Are you still calling it ***Untitled***? That's so lame, Jed."

I frowned. "I am going to the bar. Do you want anything?" I asked.

"No." He shook his head and seated himself at the opposite end of the semicircle-shaped corner booth that I held for the group. "I'm not drinking tonight. I can't afford shit, because the internship at Truffle does not pay."

"Don't forget to thank them again for that, Yost. It's good experience." He glared at me hard. "Six years ago I was miserable too," I said.

"Yeah. Don't give me that whole 'my rich daddy forced me to work every summer' sob story again. It's too old."

"Fine. Whatever. I'm going to get myself a martini."

While I was at the bar, Makiko and Beatrice arrived. I could smell Beatrice from ten feet away. I got beers for them and went back to the table. "Here, ladies. Whew! Beatrice!"

She blushed. "I overdid it at the store. I'm in the market for a new perfume."

"Yuck," Makiko said. "It's girly-girl nonsense." Makiko was being a hypocrite, as she was more likely to be in couture than Dean or I. "Where's Dean?"

"He's coming."

"Yeah, he's coming on YOU," Makiko said.

I dropped the beers for the "ladies" on the table and took back my spot at the booth. "Nah, but I did come in your girlfriend." Beatrice blushed again. "Sorry, babe." I took a gulp of my martini.

"Can we save the debauchery for later, guys?" Yost asked. "I was led to believe that we were here to support and advise Jed as fellow writers."

Makiko leaned across the table to face Yost. "You will never finish anything unless you can embrace all sides of your sexuality."

"Whatever. That's just bones, dear. An old argument. I don't need to experience anal sex in order to be capable of writing a great story. I need to read, read, and then read some more."

Makiko scoffed. "That's a cliché!"

"It's a cliché, but it's true," Yost said.

"I read too, but there's more to it," Makiko said. "A writer without worldly experience is like a sanitation worker without a truck. Just as he uses his truck to house all the trash, you need to use worldly experience to accomplish your goal. You have insufficient experience to draw upon, and that's why you can't finish a chapter." Beatrice gave me a very confused look. Makiko's metaphor didn't make any sense.

"No. I don't buy it." He paused. "That's the reason why your poetry is published by 'Truffle.' You are not good enough and are in no position to give this sort of advice," Yost said bitterly.

I was tempted to remind him that he was the only person at the table who had not sold a text to date. I gulped the rest of my martini. "Okay. This is not the point of our gathering," I said. The cocktail waitress appeared. I held up my glass and mouthed the word "another."

"This is so typical," Beatrice said. She pushed the beer across the table. "You can't handle a serious situation. Makiko and Yost are trying to re-hash a recurring argument, and . . . I don't drink beer."

"Exactly," Yost said. "That's why your new book is fucked and has no real title. You don't listen to us."

"I do."

"No, you don't," Makiko said. "We told you that ***Untitled*** was not going to work when you gave us the outline."

"Dean supported me. He—"

Yost cut me off. "When Dean gets here, he will blow smoke up your ass yet again."

Makiko cackled. "He'll give you a fucking rim job too."

"That's all that you are getting out of this group," Yost said.

Makiko and Beatrice nodded. "You can't take an ill-conceived idea and execute it half-assed," Beatrice added.

"Exactly," Yost said. "It doesn't work. You aren't serious enough."

"So I should dump it?"

"Yes," the three of them said in unison.

"Please. I can't read this shit anymore!" Makiko said. "It's such a cliché."

My second drink arrived. "Get me one of those," Beatrice said. "I'm the one who got you into martinis, remember?" I didn't, but nodded and grinned at her nonetheless. (Incidentally, it was probably Dean. I met Dean in 1997, and we did plenty of drinking those first few years. I dated Beatrice for seven strange months in 2001.) "Let's be constructive for a moment," she said. "You told us all about Shane Lasch."

"Yes. That was a hoot," Makiko said.

Yost went stone-faced and decided to hold court with his point of view at this stage. "Shane can represent a point of view. By himself, he is not novel at all. He's a crazy protagonist. If you chose a first-person narrative, where the reader can quickly gather that he or she should be skeptical of the narrator, then it would not be original. That's been done before. I can think of at least a half-dozen examples off the top of my head. As I said, he could be a point of view, or an element of a larger work. Shane is not a novel. It's not even viable as a short story."

"I disagree on your last point, Yost," Beatrice said. "It could work as a short story, if Jed makes it ambiguous. Is Shane delusional, or does the destroyer exist? Does the destroyer truly compel Shane to mutilate himself?"

I laughed. "I didn't even think of that angle from the real life incident. He probably believes that I psychically compelled him to do that. I'll keep that in mind if I get to interview him."

"Yes, you need to do that. You need to take, take, take, and then take some more. Suck the information out of him like it's blood. Be a vampire," Makiko said.

"And then throw him away like a used condom, girlfriend!" Dean yelled. He stood at the head of our table.

"Hey, buddy. Take a seat. We'll get you a drink," I said. Yost scoffed and mimicked "girlfriend" under his breath. I moved closer to Makiko and Dean sat at the end.

"I want a dry vodka martini," he said.

"The cocktail waitress will be back in a minute."

"Cool. Do you have a title yet? I read it again, and I like it," Dean said.

"How so?"

"Umm. It's good," he said. Yost groaned, but Dean pretended not to notice. "It's more experimental."

"Yeah," Makiko said. "That sums it up."

I didn't have the energy to defend Dean, so I paid for his drinks instead. Dean continued to defend ***Untitled*** by describing the plot.

"Good book report, dude," Yost said. "It's so good and experimental." Makiko laughed. "She agrees," he added.

"Does anybody have anything else to talk about? Projects? Life? Telepathic assassins? Oh, wait. We already covered that one," Makiko said.

The table went silent, so I switched gears. "Yes. I have a suggestion for you, Yost. When I went to your school, Professor Grayson did an excellent fiction workshop. I was already interested in being a novelist then, but he was a big help. He is a writer's laxative."

"Excuse me?" Makiko asked. "You could have articulated that better." She paused to formulate her take. "Just as a chocolate laxative binge can loosen your bowels, he can loosen your mind."

Yost grinned. "Since I have had so much trouble crapping down the page lately, I would benefit greatly from that mental enema," he said.

"No," Beatrice said. She shook her head and giggled. "It's a class full of English majors who drink coffee by the gallon. Right? I sure that they have no problems at all when it comes to shitting!"

"Okay," I said. "Let me take another shot. When all is said and done, both Professor Grayson and a laxative will increase your load of excrement. The only difference is that Grayson will force you to eat shit, but a big old steaming pile of poop won't force you to do a thing but flush the toilet."

That's a good spot to end. As usual, the conversation petered out. They made their point, and I need to think.

From the Journal of Margaret Telfer

June 18, 2003

Today was so much fun. I broke up with Barry. We had lunch at the Banyon's Steakhouse in Chelsea. He didn't eat and went to the bathroom, coming back with a telltale powder trail below his nostrils. I told him it was over.

After work, I went to drink myself into oblivion at Maran. There were some highly unpleasant kids there. I sat in the booth next to them and guzzled Chardonnay while I eavesdropped.

They were all writers. I recognized Makiko Lee and finally got confirmation that she's a lesbian. I didn't even know that old burnout was still in New York. Back in the day, that might have made the gossip column. My company published her terrible novel eight years ago, and it did not sell.

The only one there who said anything intelligent was this kid named Yost. I didn't catch his last name, but I need to keep my eye out for him. I think he's still in school, but he's a sharp little bastard.

From Makiko's Diary/Poetry Sketchbook

June 18, 2003

Beatrice is the most fucked-up girl I've ever dated. She still wants to be with Shane, her pretty boy ex. Bea is always telling me that she's so glad that he stays single. She's pleased that he "plays the field." Does that mean that she thinks he'll try to get back with her when he feels like it's time to settle down? I wish I were a gay man. Men just fuck, and they don't speak in code.

We hung out with Shane and his faggot friends at this too-expensive bar in midtown. Are we a coven of writers? Hah! That's so dramatic. We'd be a coven of gay writers, except for that troll Yost. At least Jed lets men suck his cock now and again. I wonder if he ever tried to smoke some pole.

Okay. Time for poetry:

"I want a cock"

I want a cock and rocks.
I want to come on her blouse.
And live in fine house.

Men got it best.
Porn is made to pass their test
They get jobs that pay the best

The bearers of cocks and rocks rule.
They get to come every time and act like a fool.
We're on the outside looking in and can only drool.

Ah, yes! Another lousy poem! More scraps for my junkyard! Time to cut and paste!

From the Literary Exercises/Journal of Jed Haele

June 20, 2003

Untitled is dead. Long live ***Untitled 2: the Destroyers***!

In all seriousness, the novel's title will contain some variation of the word "destroyer." Shane's name will be Sean in the book. Sean will think others are destroyers, and then he will partially destroy himself.

I haven't heard from Shane yet, but I know that I will.

I solved the output problem. Simon came up with a great idea when I called him before. He's a trip. He was on his way out of his apartment and must have been half-naked with flyers and headshots among other things lying about as he prepared for a screening of ***Sorority Road Trip***. He got his client, Brooke Easton, a small supporting role in the movie. In spite of everything, he was lucid and his suggestion was gold.

"Installments. You can get something out there in weeks, or even days. You'll probably hook even more readers."

"I need to —"

"You need to end each installment with a cliffhanger."

I paused for a split second to ponder the creative compromise this requires. "Have you read me?"

He sighed. "Of course."

"Don't you think that would compromise my writing style? I'm writing a novel, not an action movie screenplay where something blows up every fifteen minutes and—" He abruptly put me on hold.

Then, he continued. "Just leave them wanting more."

"More?"

"Exactly." He ended the conversation. I checked my e-mail repeatedly before making dinner as I plotted my strategy for ***Destroyer*** (the working title for today).

Later in the evening, I posted the following text on the home page of the jedhaele.com website:

The wait is almost over, and my next project will commence one week from tonight. It will unfold one chapter at a time. Each new chapter will heighten the tension and suspense as you discover the latest evolution in excitement and terror:

"I'm moving to Cali next week, so—"

"You need summer clothes there all year round. You'd need them if you stayed here too. Summer is coming. It gets hot and loud, and people get into fights on the streets. It's a fucking riot."

"A riot?"

"Yeah, bub. More so every year. It seems."

Don't you look at me like that!" he said, louder.

"Like that?" Darren asked. "It's the only reasonable way to respond. You just called my friend a serial killer based on an . . . observation?"

"This is more than an observation! I experienced it myself. I experienced his power! His gruesome . . ."

"He's a beast!"

"He can control you minds!"

"He . . . He . . . He . . . He can kill you all with his mind!"

"It will all end, because of people like them."

"DESTROYER!"

Coming Friday June 27, 2003.

Your mind will never be the same.

I've fictionalized Dean into Darren before, but never myself. I want a name that starts with a "J." Joshua, Jason, Johnny, Joe, Jaden, Jose, Julian?

I'm going to write this thing whether I hear from Shane or not. The first chapter will be very quiet and subdued. It might not draw in more readers, but current subscribers will not be able to stand the tension, because they will know something freaky is on the way. The dialogue from the preview above will belong to a later chapter. I'm not going to outline this thing. I'm going to take a chance and write with a new mantra: Less rules, more adaptation.

Juan, Jorge, Javier (So many male Spanish names start with "J." I wonder why.), Justin, Jeremy, Jasper, Jimmy? Making lists is boring. I'll choose between Jaden, Jason, and Julian. Maybe I can let the subscribers vote. That'll make them feel like they are part of the process and get them more excited.

On second thought, that's a lame idea because that would set a precedent. Next thing I know, they'll want to vote to dictate plot twists. It's a slippery slope!

June 24

I have a first draft of chapter one. All of Sean's activities are regimented, and he's "***fanatically opposed to deviations from his long set habits: His alarm clock wakes him at 7:00 every morning, including Saturday and Sunday. He endures a brutal exercise regimen immediately thereafter for exactly one half hour.***" Yeah, Sean is latently gay. Mental note: BE SUBTLE ABOUT SEAN'S HOMOSEXUALITY.

At the end of the chapter, he sees Julian for the first time on a crosstown bus during his lunch hour. Julian's eyes fix on Sean's like a death grip. The chapter ends with dialogue between a buff drag queen and another passenger that indicates a fight is about to break out between them.

June 25

Of course, I changed the chapter. The ending now takes place on a sparsely filled Q60 bus en route to Queens around midnight. Sean had to stay at work until late, so he's annoyed because his "***regimented schedule***" is disturbed.

I improved the specificity of the combatants, as well. One is a sloppy aging drag queen who's "***taking the bus in the wrong direction. His tight scaly skirt smothered his blubbery thighs, and those garish hot pink press-on nails hung loosely off each digit.***" The other is a German tourist whose "***angular face and excellently sculpted frame was marred by a myriad of acne scars across his cheeks and forehead.***"

Now, it's Janine's turn.

By the way, Julian is an alien. This is my tentative plan for the end game, but I'll keep the telepathic who triggers violence thing going for a while. I'm going to surprise everyone, including my writer friends with the twist. I already have a cool image for a future chapter, where Sean slaps Julian across the face and he bleeds white blood. Instead of making him a superhuman "destroyer" who was created by man (this is the type of sci-fi aesthetic I want to avoid), he'll be an "other" from elsewhere that conceivably could exist. In short, no creature in this book will be earth-based or the result of an experiment.

Sean will misunderstand the alien and ultimately mutilate himself because of ignorance and fear. The alien does not cause fights. Rather, he has acute psychic abilities and can sense the tension between the Kraut and the Drag Queen before their fight erupts. Thus, his psychic powers draw him to spots where violence will shortly erupt. Sean's injury and subsequent discovery of the alien's true nature will be the impetus for his redemption.

From the Journal of Hunter

June 24, 2003

Lately, when I think about how it went bad, I recall the summer of 1989. There were days where I drove through the seedy part of Santa Monica Boulevard over and over and observed those lost souls. The hookers, pimps, perverts, and dealers were gray and red with some black teeth peppering fake smiles.

My fresh license rested on the newly re-upholstered passenger seat of my pink car. My body was almost pristine, except for the smallest scar from a cigarette burn. That tiny flesh-colored scar has grown darker.

Weeks or months later, I wore an aqua Versace shirt to Deena's sixteenth birthday party. I didn't pace myself very well and landed on a couch with a shot in hand. I slowly drooled Bacardi 151 down the front of my shirt. Once it reached the bottom of my shirt, the joint I held by my crotch ignited the shirt.

They noticed it before me. The slender line of fire went up to my neck. Someone lunged at me with a blanket.

My shirt split across the front, and I wasn't wearing a bra, so I was suddenly very popular. "You should be in fashion," a queen who snuck in remarked. He lovingly fingered the charred panels.

After I passed out (I always pass out) and recovered, my shirt was crudely sewn up, but I had barfed on it, probably after it was mended.

From the Literary Exercises/Journal of Jed Haele

June 29, 2003

I brought the chapter to a screening last night to show Simon. Simon was depressed and down. "I can't pull this off," he sobbed to me in a corner of an empty room in the producer's Westchester mansion. What happened to his confidence? He rambled and only intermittently got to the point. "Brooke is so fat now. It's "finger down the throat" time for her. I swear to God. It is. They're all so fat! My clients! Especially Brooke! God damn it! She's in a movie that's going to be a hit! Why is she so fat NOW!"

"Relax, Simon," I enunciated the syllables.

"She got cut to death. The producer is trying to humiliate me. Fucking cock-sucking bastard. With a high-pitched fucking Amadeus laugh."

I laughed. "You'd want to rip out his larynx, right?"

"Cock-sucker," he mouthed grimly. "Rip his fucking larynx out. And dunk his cunt wife's head in the tar pits next time I'm in L.A."

"Regardless, it's less than a week away."

"Yep. July 4, 2003, is the release date for both ***Sorority Road Trip*** and ***Dinosaur Attack 2: Volcano Island.*** Nobody's fooling themselves. It's no contest, but this producer thinks we will make a dent in the dinosaur coin."

"The one who owns this house?"

"Yeah. He's already pushing for a sequel, because this one cost next to nothing. Brooke might get a bigger role next time if she loses weight, gives him head, and agrees to show her tits again. He alludes to all three whenever he calls me. It's funny, because he calls me at least three times a week because the release date is coming up, and with each conversation, he's worked in all three requirements in new and amusing ways." He sighed. "That's what makes you so lucky. You're an entrepreneur. You are in charge." I pulled the pages out of my jacket, and he smiled weakly. "I got the free first chapter from Janine already. You got my thirty bucks for the rest, but—"

I cut him off. "I came up with that idea on my own. Two-thirds have already signed up to pay for the rest of the novel, and most of the rest should by the eleventh. You don't have to worry about it. My friends get the book for free. Remember?"

He continued, as if I didn't interrupt him and didn't absorb what I said. "It's not good yet. You know that, right?" he said. I nodded, hesitantly. "It has to get better, or else it will suck."

"Sure, but there's more reward than risk. Each chapter is another opportunity to blow them away. I'll keep surprising them."

He shook his head and stared me in the eye. "You are fucking up. You didn't leave them wanting more. You have to get your shit together, deliver something good in the next chapter, or else these Internet geeks are going to rip you a new one." He took a deep breath and exhaled hard. "Or worse, they won't subscribe next time."

"It's going to pick up. I promise."

"Okay. I don't want you to turn into a lightweight. You know how to do this. Okay? Stop fucking around."

Electronic music from the film's soundtrack blasted through the house. "Want to go back to the party? Brooke might be eating," I suggested.

Simon mock-bolted. He's hardly anorexic anymore himself. He stopped by the door and asked, "Are you really going to bang out fifteen pages twice a month like clockwork?"

Is the plan sustainable? No, but I'm going to shift the schedule a bit to make it possible and release my chapters on Wednesday while working as if the previous Friday is the deadline because that gives me Monday and Tuesday to polish. I'll also make some of the breaks between chapters three weeks instead of two. And then, there is ***Untitled***.

"I'll throw ***Untitled*** out there as a cheaper novel to satiate them when I need a month or two." I approached him and added, "I have no reserves aside from that."

"Really? You're a writer."

"Actually, you're right. I have a short story called 'Creamed.' It's about a deadly cream."

"That kills?"

I smirked. "Yeah. That's what deadly means." We both laughed. "But there is a party tonight, and chunky butt needs her cocaine, right?" I asked.

"Oh Jesus! I almost forgot," he said and then bolted for real.

June 30, 2003

I never write this early but I got a call from Simon before sunrise, and he invited me to the premiere of ***Sorority Road Trip*** tonight. "I got two extra tickets to the premiere. Can you come?" That's exactly how he started the conversation. It wasn't even six yet.

"I'm working, but I guess so. Dean might be game."

"I'm sure he will be."

I couldn't get back to sleep after that, so I lazily worked on the chapter. I waited until a decent hour and called Dean. He was quite enthusiastic. "Dude. It's not your first premiere," I said soberly.

"Yeah, but this is a big movie! People will recognize us!"

"I doubt it. You were on a show that less than half a million people watched, and an audience of thousands reads me."

"What about the ***Wired*** article?"

"Yeah," was all I could muster. It was still too early in the day to discuss my only press to date. I was only one of the "25 Up and Coming Innovators in Internet Marketing" they covered.

(Later)

Dean, in his desperation, decided that we needed to go to Soho to buy new clothes for the premiere. "You do realize that you are not in the film," I said to him when he arrived at my apartment and presented this notion to me at my door as follows: "We need new clothes now! There'll be stars there! Fuck! C'mon, bitch! Let's go to Soho!" He took a breath and continued, "I'm jazzed! I'm hot! We have to get fabulous!" Okay, this was very out of character for Dean. He's rarely swishy like that.

"What is up with you?" I asked.

He shook his head. "C'mon, bitch. We need to go!" He grabbed my arm and literally pulled me out the door.

"Okay. Let's spend the rest of your money!" I hesitated at the door, and he pulled harder. "Will you hold up for a moment? I need to lock my door."

Thankfully, I convinced him to go uptown. I hate Soho. I bought a black silk shirt and will pair it with my salt-and-pepper–colored jeans and a red leather jacket. Dean bought a light blue suit. It was fitted, but looked very casual. He was quite enthusiastic. "Are you high today?" I asked when we compared purchases at Club Cafe. I noticed that his knee was shaking.

"Yes," he said. "I'm running out of money fast, Jed."

I think that I might have a new freeloading roommate very soon. Oh well, there's no time to worry about that now. I need to get ready for the party.

July 1

The premiere was at the new multiplex in Times Square. It was a hot night, and they closed off the entire street. Dean and I arrived late and did the red carpet together. Of the roughly seventy-five to one hundred photographers, I would say a half dozen recognized me, and about three times as many recognized Dean. "I'm working on a new novel!" I yelled over the flashbulbs and the fans who squealed over our predecessor on the red carpet (one of the film's three leads) as well as our successor (the boyfriend of one of the other leads who discreetly arrived separately from her). Yes, I was jealous. I wanted them to squeal for me. I'm sort of kind of famous! Damn it!

Once we got inside, I stared down dozens of teen tarts with fake tits among the producers, wives, agents, and lecherous older male B-list actors who were trolling for teen tarts. Was this a premiere, or a utopian singles bar for dirty old men?

I waded through these people in the lobby for what felt like hours alongside Dean, but his desperate grins at producers and attempts at small talk with agents saddened me. His desperation reeked worse than the filthy street outside.

We separated, and I rode the elevator upstairs to the third floor. The theater level wasn't as crowded, and an open bar was set up near the concession stand. Naturally, the producers flocked to it. I ordered a martini and immediately got attention from one of them. "Jed Haele." He pronounced my name properly. "I'm Troy Lainer. Your books are great. My son quotes them at the dinner table." He paused between each sentence and spoke in a grim monotone.

"I'm not doing any screenplays, but I appreciate your interest." That's my way of saying that the novels are not for sale. I use the exact same phrase every time. I anticipated that I would need to say the line at least a dozen times at the premiere, so I had practiced it beforehand in the mirror.

He shook his head and spoke much more forcefully. "You keep this up, and people will stop asking!" He paused and gave me a mean look. "Fuck you!" he yelled, strutting to the theater.

I guzzled my beer and got another. Another one approached me. "Troy is an asshole. I'm Jared Berling," he said with a raspy voice. He was younger. He wore the same suit as Dean, but in dark gray. "I don't know how he even got invited. I'm one of the producers of the film."

"Sorority whatever the fuck."

He grinned. "Yes, I know. It is exploitation, and we'll probably get the chance to turn it into a franchise and run it into the ground with a dozen sequels. It's lovely, but I'm also interested in you."

"Really?"

"I have a mantra, Jed. Would you like me to share it with you?"

"Sure."

"With bitterness and rage I proceed," he said sternly, with a sudden grave expression on his face.

"That's creepy."

He shook his head and smiled. "Yeah, it is. You don't want to sell your novels or adapt them to screenplays, but you should." He grabbed my wrist and spoke softly. "It might make you bitter, and you might feel rage when you watch a ninety-five–minute long bastardization of your text on the big screen, but it will draw more people back to the original novel, and then you'll thank me for grabbing your arm like this." His eyes were dark and cold, and his skin was freshly scrubbed and clear.

"I'm not doing any screenplays, but I appreciate your interest," I said and started to walk away.

"Give me another shot, Jed." I turned back around. "Here's my assessment of your novel's prospects for the silver screen. ***Shelby*** won't work." I nodded. At least he was smart enough to realize that, and I have to give him credit for it. "On the other hand, a solid screenwriter could congeal ***Dance of the Damned***, and we could deliver a solid independent film. All the gender issues would scare off a major studio, but an independently produced and financed film could be excellent. Good reviews would make it a hit, and the DVD sales would be solid because of your loyal and growing fan base. I do have a screenwriter in mind, as well as a director. I am going to make a ton of cash off 'Sorority whatever the fuck.'" He paused and grinned hard. I imagined his lip tearing in the middle from the excessive stretching. "This could work so well for both of us." He paused. "I know that you stonewall us. May I ask you why?" He was better than average at this.

"I own my work and make plenty of money off of it, but I am not greedy. I work in my small niche of fiction, and I am happy. Also, I am concerned that a bad adaptation would turn my readers off to future novels."

"Let me level with you. I want an excellent indie film credit on my resume so I can get respect from better filmmakers and actors. ***Sorority Road Trip*** is mid-level trash, and I want to be a major producer. I need to make a 'film.'"

"Jed," I heard Dean yell from a few feet away.

"Here comes your friend. I loved his show, but reality is not . . ."

Dean tapped my shoulder. "This is Dean," I said.

"Jared Berling. It's nice to meet you, Dean. Please enjoy the film." He slipped a card to me. "Let's talk some more," he said and sauntered toward the theater.

I shuddered. "I need to take a shower."

"What's wrong?"

"Let's just say that I'm glad you showed up when you did. Satan was about to describe how his screenwriter would bludgeon one of my novels. Fortunately, his fear of conversing with a reality show contestant scared him away. Like garlic and Dracula. You know?"

"That reminds me. Have you seen Simon?"

"That's really funny, Dean."

"I'm sorry, but—"

I cut him off. "Simon means well. He's just overwhelmed." Dean and I had another free drink and quietly waited for him.

Simon looked exhausted as he came up the escalator. He had not shaved, and his face was puffy and white. I considered asking him about this, but then realized that he wasn't sleeping due to the stress of the film's imminent release date.

"Dean and Jed. I'm so glad that I could get my two celebrity friends to show up for this. It's a fucking coup! My boss shit his pants when I told him!"

"I'm going to be a writer too," Dean said. I groaned. Dean brought this up a few weeks ago. I grimly suggested that he keep a journal and read. I hoped that it would be a quickly discarded notion. "I'm going to start a journal any day now," he added. At least he's stalling. That's always a good sign that someone's not too serious.

"Who has time to keep a fucking journal?" Simon asked. He cocked his head and frowned his chapped lips.

"I do."

"I will," Dean said with too much conviction.

"You do another red carpet with Dean, and they'll think you're a fucking faggot too," Simon said.

I turned to Dean. He was not amused. "Dean. Calm down. He's bi."

Simon scoffed. "Keep quiet about that. This is the second most homophobic industry around right now."

Before I could find out which industry was number one, he rushed us to the theater. "I have to sit with Brooke!" he yelled and paced ahead of us.

They showed the film on the two largest screens simultaneously. Since I had already seen it, I spent most of the screening around the open bar. I chatted with some of the bored aging actors. I wanted to know how they got their invitations, since their presence seemed so incongruous. My suspicions were correct about their interest in bagging teen tarts. "My agent is the best. He gets me tickets to all the teen flick premieres, and I get head every time," one of them said. I didn't recognize him, but he was old enough to be my father.

I skipped the party afterward. I did not want to contend with sales pitches from drunk and/or high producers and really did not want to see nineteen-year-olds giving aging actors head every time I went to the restroom to take a leak. Dean and Simon went together, and I hope that they bonded.

Absent a late night at said party I still slept until noon and have not worked on the chapter at all today.

July 2, 2003

I was halfway through a draft that sucked when I got this e-mail from Shane Lasch:

From: mistaman@axl.com
To: zedsdeadjed@oroboros.com
Subject: Fuck You
Date: Wednesday, 2 July 2003 07:07:06

I know why you gave me this. You knew that I wouldn't be able to resist. Now you have my e-mail address, and no matter where I go, every time I sign onto a computer, you may be there.

I could resist again and insist upon the truth, but what would that get me? However, if I decide to play into his accusation and pretend that I am this "Destroyer," then I could get more material for my book. I sent the following text in response: ***"I am Jed Hell, and I will speak candidly now if you wish. How about the diner across from the bar (you know which bar) tomorrow, around six?"***

From the Journal of Hunter

July 1, 2003

You could say that it's terminal, or that I'm terminal, and I would say that more likely than not you're right. I'm indifferent to death now. I honestly don't care. Resignation is spooky. Years ago, when I had a chance of recovering, I truly feared death. I did not want to die. I'm truly indifferent now, and it is quite eerie.

July 2, 2003

When Shane called me, his voice sounded different. It was hollow and emotionless, almost like a crisp and clear computer voice. He wanted Clea's number. I couldn't find it, so he hung up on me.

July 3, 2003

The hobo who might read this journal, if he finds it when he rummages through the landfill, where it'll likely wind up when they throw it all away, will not understand me. He won't know what happened to me if I don't explain.

My real name is Carla Hunt. When I die, I'll be thirty-two years old. My birthday was a month ago, and my boyfriend broke up with me shortly before it. It's a few weeks later now, and that's how long it takes to die. I will probably swallow or inject enough poison today or tomorrow, because I have to.

It's a strategic move, if you can believe it. I'm cutting my losses. Slow torture versus a quick end to the pain? It's my choice. All I can do when I think about it is exhale hard and try to decide on the ideal hour of the day.

I just realized that this is my suicide note.

From the Literary Exercises/Journal of Jed Haele

July 3, 2003

When Shane appeared, of course, I intended to look down at his right hand before anything, but I did not notice him initially because he had lost at least fifteen pounds and was very pale.

He moved like a specter in pursuit of my table, from one table to the next, confused and disheveled. He passed my table twice and did not recognize me. "Shane," I hollered. He turned and held up his right "hand."

A white fingerless glove molded his mangled "hand" into a paddle-like enclosure. "My new hand will be metal and cost $35,000," he said. He sat down across from me and rested it on the checkered tablecloth.

"I am choosing to be candid now, because your persistence and commitment to your belief is so refreshing," I said. He grimaced and pulled off his black cowboy hat, seething. "Is this about the money? For your hand?" He shook his head dismissively. "Wow. Okay, then I suppose you've come here to tell me off again."

He scoffed. "Will I be more like you then?"

"When?"

"When I get my new hand."

This really irritated me because the new iteration of his lunacy conflicted with my plan for the book. I tried to shut this notion down to redirect his delusions in a direction that suited my needs better. "No. I'm not modified like that. I was born this way. You can't be like me, no matter how hard you try."

"On some level I do envy that you have a power, but I would never want to be like you. I want a power that could save people, not destroy them."

"Save who?" I asked slyly.

Shane went stone faced and raised his hand into the air. He pulled the glove off to reveal foam rubber. He ripped off the foam and squished it into his pocket, revealing the remnants of his hand. The people at nearby tables gasped, and a passing waitress dropped her tray of plates. They fell to the floor and made a crunchy crash.

I couldn't look away from the meat as he dropped his arm back down on the table. Bandages covered the end of his wrist, but bloodstains peaked out through the bandages. Beneath the bandages was open, wounded flesh.

I was mesmerized. "You relinquish some control with this candor," he suggested. He smiled. "And then, I can win," he concluded confidently. He stood up, walked a few steps, and paused. He turned to say, "Tell Dean that I say hi," and then left.

In his warped mind, I suspect Shane believes that he gained an advantage over me through this show-and-tell session. In my own warped mind, this encounter just confirms that I read him right when I decided to make him my subject. The second chapter will write itself, and I expect that the subsequent chapters will fall into place nicely.

There are two problems. One is an enigma. His attitude toward the $35,000 cost for the new hand was remarkably blasé. I still think he wants money from me. The other issue is the new metallic hand itself. It's at odds with the science fiction model I want to work with later on. I don't want to write about modified human beings when I get deeper into the novel, and that's what Shane is doing. I have to resolve the latter problem, and fast.

July 4, 2003

Shane/Sean wishes that he was born modified, and this is an underlying motivation for the mutilation sequence. Shane/Sean's mind is too small to understand that the modification he seeks will not accomplish this. He's just read too many comic books. I can set this up through flashbacks, possibly in the current chapter. That's a problem with writing like this. I wind up locked into events for later on, because I choose to set them up now.

Another problem is the lukewarm response to the first chapter. The plan was to make it a freebie and access to the second chapter would be my payday. As expected, most have signed up (1785 out of 1903 at last count), but there have been zero new subscribers. In addition, I've already received responses from my writing buddies, and well . . . here are excerpts.

Beatrice:

"[General comments about how it's really good and interesting] . . . it's mostly exposition so far, so it's hard to judge. I have no clue where you're going with this. Should I? The conclusion of the chapter comes out of nowhere, and it ends too abruptly."

Yost:

"I'm not sure that you edited it. Are you going to do so later on? As it stands now, too much of the text seems extraneous. Based upon my reading, the plot starts on the last page."

Makiko:

"This is not pleasing anybody. It doesn't have the gore and bizarre plot points that would satisfy your internet subscribers, and it doesn't have any of the elements that would work for hard-copy publishing."

My God! These are my colleagues? What will the other, less-trained readers think?

I absolutely cannot release ***Untitled*** now to buy time if I run into trouble with ***Shane the Pain*** (the latest working title). I have nimbly avoided title issues so far with everyone, somehow. If people are not enjoying ***Shane the Pain***, then I can't release another weak text, even if it is at a big discount. That's a waste of eight months of work. Now I'm locked into the tight schedule for ***Shane the Pain***, without any respite.

The second chapter is now shaky, because I am losing my confidence. There absolutely is flop-sweat at this stage. The fight sequence has a rambunctious quality to it. It's bloody and involves many torn sequins. They lunge back and forth in rhythm with the bus driver's fits and stops as the driver maneuvers among the bumps in the road: ***"The tourist grumbled and coughed on the floor. His arm was sore and bleeding from the impact of the rings. The other struggled to hold his torn dress together because of his overworked thong and the spillage! He cursed in a much deeper voice, and went back for more!"***

Next up, I have to fill in some more back-story and crap out some secondary plot to kill time before he sees Julian appear around another fight. After the second fight, he will become suspicious and talk to people about it. Of course, everybody will think that he's demented.

July 5

I went to my parents' house yesterday for their July 4th barbeque. I coerced Janine and Dean into tagging along. I have meant to invite her to some function for a while because we have been working together now for almost two years. This felt like a good opportunity and it got us out of town for the day. She had never been out to Port Jefferson before either. I invited her with the best of intentions, but it was very unpleasant.

We took the LIRR after lunch. Janine got restless after a half hour. "Why are you dressed like a porn star?" she asked. I wore a tight aqua shirt with "Summer Fun" embossed in dark blue across it, and white gym shorts.

"It's my color scheme for today. Get over it."

"He's trying to look sexy for his parents," Dean said. Janine cackled and I cringed.

"Did you do this every day when you went to NYU?" she asked.

"Oh God no." I scoffed. "They plucked from their money tree and had me stay at the dorms."

Janine laughed. "I don't think you minded it all that much, Jed."

I glared at her through my sunglasses. "I didn't, but that's not the point." She scrunched her brow. "Well, you know what I do, Janine. Yes, I know I sound like the ungrateful spoiled spawn of privilege here, but this was all calculated on their part. It's really only succession planning. They sent me to school, gave me this overpaid job in the salt mine that is their Time's Square store to groom me to work in his office. Eventually I'll replace him and run his little fast food empire so they can retire to California."

"They sound lovely," she said sarcastically.

"The scary part is the stroke hasn't slowed her down one bit. If anything, it has made her worse," Dean said.

"Yeah, her speech recovered ahead of schedule. She's too mean to not speak well. I swear it's like she had a choice between her speech and mobility, and she picked speech.

We got there a half hour later. Chester was too lazy to pick us up so we took a cab. Janine and Dean sat in the back seat and took in the scenery. It was so bright and they were spellbound when we took the road by the water.

We pulled into the cul de sac shortly after, and I pointed at the large house at the end of the block. Between the stark white stucco and the sun at its apex on this very clear day, it resembled the images of heaven from the movies, minus the clouds. I felt ill.

"It's so different from the other houses," Janine said. "It's so white."

"You do not even want to know how much they spent to modify it like that."

The cab dropped us at the curb and I led them up the walkway lined with the custom-made white lights that glow blue at night. We went inside, and it smelled from recent construction. The staircase still looked messy, but the chair lift looked functional.

"That really fucked up the carpet," Dean said.

Janine turned to look at the dining room to the left and the kitchen beyond it. "Still. Wow!" she said. "I love those black chairs."

"Watch out for the corners of the table. They can cut you," Dean said.

I paced ahead of them through the hall, the living room, and stopped at the glass doors to the pool. Mom gripped her cane tightly with her right arm as she stood by Dad at the grill. "They waste no time," I said to myself. They caught up; I put my game face on and opened the door. My parents did their standard creepy smile as we approached, and my dad returned his attention to the grill. Mom's hair was a fright. She gave Janine her hard stare. She sucked in her chubby cheeks slightly and exhaled hard while holding a slight smile. She put out her other hand.

"You're Janine. You're so . . . What's the word, Seymour?"

He looked up from the grill for a moment. "Usefull," he said.

She cackled creepily. "That's right. We have a rough time believing Jed can write all those books without SOME HELP. His spelling was always terrible."

Janine cocked her head and grinned. "He does pay well to fix his spelling AND punctuation."

"Oh, that was a bit crass of me," she said and motioned for us to go to the table. It sure was. She managed to insult both of us in one fell swoop. The scraping of the metal patio chairs as we settled in suited my irritation.

She read my displeasure so easily. "I say so because we do love Jed's little pet project so much. It gives him character and keeps him busy. So how do you like the house?"

"Oh, well we basically just ran through it, Fiona. That dining room is gorgeous. I love those chairs."

"They're oriental." Dean barely held back a cackle, and thankfully she missed that because she was still staring mostly at Janine. She sighed. "I should be better behaved. With these guests," she trailed off.

"Where's Chester?" I asked.

"He's playing video games."

Dad came over with a platter of swordfish, steaks, and a small condescending pile of hot dogs, presumably for Janine and Dean if they wished to be so tacky. "Help yourselves, kids," he said and returned to the house.

"Oh, these men!" She turned to me.

"He probably needs to make some calls. Did he tell you about the fire at the store in Chelsea?"

She nodded. "No, he's going away tomorrow and needs to pack. I'm leaving on Tuesday with Bettina."

"Where is Bettina?" I asked.

"Oh, we decided to be nice and let her spend the holiday with her family."

"That's very sweet of you, Fiona," Janine said.

Mom smiled at her. "I'm sure Jed would have you think otherwise, but I do try."

At this point Janine dug in and snagged a swordfish steak. "What's for dessert?" she asked.

"Peach pie."

Janine grimaced. "No apple pie?"

Mom grimaced. "We never have apple pie. Jed doesn't eat apples," she said, and Dean nodded. "He refuses to touch them."

"That's odd," Janine said. "Is he allergic?"

"I just don't like them. The taste, the sound they make when people eat them, their . . . everything. I don't care for them."

"Did you ever eat them?" Janine asked.

"He used to eat them," Mom said.

"But I never liked them. I don't think I've had anything with apple in it in at least ten years."

Once they were through grilling me about apples (I mean Jesus there are people who hate to eat liver or broccoli. Nobody makes a fucking federal case over it), we discussed my plan for the new book. At one point Janine offered some input and Mom barely acknowledged her. She dug the condescension in very deep when Janine persisted.

"Don't take this the wrong way, dear, but this is business, and all you do is fix his spelling and punctuation."

"Of course," Janine said, instinctively knowing she had to take that bullet.

She turned to me again. "This episodic release strategy is a major deviation, and I need to read my son's head. I need to figure out if he really has a fucking plan here." She paused and hardened her expression. "I do have my doubts."

At some point she tottered off to use the bathroom. Once she was out of view, Janine slapped the back of my head. "I'm sorry, Janine. I thought they would be nicer to a girl." I didn't think this through well. I expected them to try to be normal for her, but I think her professional obligation to me made them see her as "the help," and they behaved accordingly.

I haven't written about my parents in a while. I blew off their Memorial Day weekend shindig somehow, so I haven't been to the house since April for Chester's birthday. I know why I don't write about them. It's because doing so is just like writing reruns. They're awful, manipulative, and eerily cloistered. They aren't human anymore.

From the first Journal of Dean Bazth

July 6, 2003

I have never written a journal before, so I don't know what to write about. Oh gosh. The grammar in the second half of that last sentence was horrible. Actually, it was the sentence before that. No, it was the sentence before . . . ugh!

Okay. That was a bad start. Can I recover? Let's see. I'm writing this because of my best friend's suggestion. Jed writes novels in his spare time and sells them to an online fan base of subscribers. He makes more money from it than he does managing one of his parents' Sterling Subs restaurants. We were talking about his latest book today, and he's very optimistic. He's writing it a chapter at a time and releasing each chapter as he writes it. It's similar to what Stephen King did with ***The Green Mile***.

He distributes the novels through the Internet to an audience base he generated entirely on his own. These people are willing to pay him to read what he has to say. That's why I am writing this journal. I want to be a writer, and Jed told me that a good first step is to keep a journal of my ideas and experiences so "You will have an expanding universe of material to draw from for your texts." Jed is the coolest straight (well, mostly straight) guy I know, but when he talks about "texts," he reminds me of a lit professor.

I like that last paragraph, because I showed something about myself without telling. By now, it's clear that I'm openly gay. By saying that "Jed is the coolest straight guy I know," I imply that I am different from him. If I were straight, then I surely would have excluded the word "straight." That said, Jed is straight to the extent that he fucks women and occasionally accepts blowjobs from men. He's a Kinsey 1, I guess. I think he only accepts the blowjobs from men because they are better at it. Also, I notice he tends to accept them when he is horny and lazy. It seems more like an alternative that comes out of convenience. I think his annoying friend Simon got to do it a few times. We never do that because we are old friends and it would be weird.

I'm a Kinsey 6 gay and single. I'm also thin, with darker Eastern European features, so I got that whole young and poised to be ruggedly handsome look going. I used to be more bulky, but once you cut the carbs, it's only a matter of time until you're buying pants with a thirty-inch waist.

I got very vain around the time I came out. I lost weight and became gorgeous. I started wearing makeup (mostly just concealer at first) and wore designer clothes. Such attire is prohibitively expensive when you're a scholarship student fresh of the bus from Middle America.

The solution to this problem pushed me to lose more weight.

I became a whore. That's something few people know. I used to be a male escort. The only reminder of that past life occurs when I walk down the street and some aging old hag gives me a second look, and I wonder if I fucked her in my former life.

Of course, I didn't become a whore solely for nice clothes that made my newly toned ass look good. That's only part of it. The primary motivation was psychological. I lost my virginity to a johnnette (for reasons unrelated to the current explanation of my own personal hell, I will save an explanation for why I only had female clientele for later). This is going to sound like bullshit, but I saw prostitution as a transition or bridge between my closeted existence as a youth and full-grown independent sexuality. I was a whore and a, yes, man to Mom and Dad who would broadcast their plan for a patronizingly conventional future that entailed upright morality and breeding and eating carbs until there weren't any notches left on my belt.

I mocked their model ruthlessly, as I FUCKED women twice my age who surely had abortions if I got them pregnant. Most of them gathered that I was straight for pay and loved me for it. Since I was gay, that meant I had no hang-ups with regard to their kinkiest fetishes. The only problem I ever encountered in that area was that some women assumed that I was submissive, because I was a twink. One lady, I think her name was Terry, was excessively rude and condescending. I don't like to take directions from women in the bedroom, albeit in that profession I did have to do that to a degree. With guys, it's different. I can be submissive, but it depends on the guy. He can't be older, because I don't go for the daddy thing. It creeps me out. Terry directed me as if she was a landing strip, and I just cannot contend with that.

That's how I met Jed six years ago. I was winding down from the valium Terry had (that was the silver lining of her employ) with coffee and clove cigarettes in a booth at an all-night diner near Madison Square Garden. A pudgy-faced guy who looked younger than I did stumbled inside, drunk. He slumped down in the corner of the empty booth opposite mine. ***Beer drinking breeder***, I thought.

"Eyy!" he shouted. I exhaled my smoke angrily and nodded without looking at him. "Gimme un of em," he said.

He was aping a Southern accent. Later on, I found out that he had spent the evening at one of the only country Western–themed bars in the city. I tossed 'em at him and remarked, "You can finish them if you promise me that you won't eat a thing."

"Whaay?" he asked, drawling.

"Because you're so fucking fat and you would look so good if you lost weight." I finally turned my head to face him. I looked him in the eye. "Trust me," I added.

"Why?" he asked, dazed and confused.

I was aghast, but remained composed. I expected a fat breeder to be glad for the advice from a queen. I'm basically a chick, who's telling him what chicks dig. "Let's call it my line of work."

He smoked until my eggs and bacon arrived, and then I invited him over. "You go on a low-carb diet," I said, pointing to the plate, "and you'll get more ass than you can handle, whichever way you want to swing. You're in New York City now. This ain't no small town in whatever the fuck state you came from where all you need is a cock to get laid. The bar is raised. You'll be hot. Trust me."

"I'm a townie," he said, surprising me.

"That doesn't matter. You'll be hot."

And he is. I'm proud of my boy.

I may be a brazen and openly shallow person, but at least I'm honest. Besides, the regimen of beauty has served Jed quite well. I seriously doubt that the oafish pig that plopped its fat hairy ass in that booth opposite me six years ago would be the successful man he is today without it. Discipline is discipline, no matter what the motivation.

Has it really been almost six years?

From the Journal of Jed Haele

July 27, 1997

I don't know if there is anything going on in my life right now that will interest you. My days seem so boring and useless. The notion that one could learn a lesson from reading about them strikes me as quite absurd. I must be one of the most boring and uninteresting people alive right now.

Having spent the last two months alternating between rotting away in this house and working at my dead-end job at the local multiplex, I can make this claim on a daily basis. Earlier today, I imagined how I could commence a conversation with one of my "acquaintances" at school in the fall by saying, "Now that I've done the dead-end job thing . . ."

I don't even know why I work this stupid job. I guess I figured it would get me out of the house and help me meet cool people and work at night. I like working at night, but the people there are depressing. They're kind of trashy and mostly commute from the south shore, and they hate me because I have money.

Can this hopeless summer be fixed? Have I hit rock bottom yet?

I can feel your excitement already. So why am I starting a journal? I want to take action, and I want to be better. I hope that specifics materialize as I write more. Besides, just when you think it's safe to declare my experience trite and insipid, I'll do something to surprise you.

July 29

Today I woke up at 1:30. That was fifteen minutes ago. No work means that I get to sleep in very late. Since I got up at 1:30, I must have done my weekly Tuesday night shift at the cinema last night.

I read ***Girl, Interrupted.*** It was disturbing, yet powerful. The author depicts herself as a spoiled lazy young adult who is driving herself crazy. This is the side I have shown so far in this journal. I am a lazy spoiled brat who is driving himself crazy.

sO ANYWAYS, I FEEL HORRIBLE, AND GUILTY AND SHITTY, AND i HATE EVERYTHING BECAuse it all sucks, and I hit my caps lock just now, and I'm not fixing it because who cares? This is just too lousy.

(Six hours later)

I feel like I am grinding away metal at this point. How long can someone be miserable? Will there come a point where my misery becomes self-destructive? Am I destroying myself with all of this? Oh wait, I forgot about how healthy I am. My vital signs are great, and I stay away from all drugs. My body is so healthy. Maybe I am destroying my mind. I don't know where that grinding metal statement came from or its relevance to this paragraph. It's probably something from my subconscious that I'll need to think about. Grinding away metal? Hmm?

(Five minutes later)

"Aliens" Ripley is anxiously driving that truck thing away from the aliens really fast after a battle. When they are very much in the clear, Michael Biehn's character says that she is just grinding away metal at that point, and he eases her hand off the accelerator. That's a cinematic metaphor for my suffering!

July 29

I was so self-indulgent yesterday. In the same vein, I composed some poetry:

"Prayer for the Dying"

And he could not breathe anymore,
because there was no more clean air.
And he could not dream anymore,
because his brain had turned to rot.
And he could not see anymore,
because he would not open his eyes.
And he couldn't cry anymore,
because there was no one left to dry his tears.
And he could not live anymore,
because there was no heart left to beat.

September 15, 1997

I wrote a short story. Thus, the six-week gap! "Advent" is a comical account of humans making contact with aliens. It is the best thing I have written so far. It is my only completed work. In spite of its short length, the story packs quite a thrilling punch. I am quite proud of it. I made it an icon on my computer, because I want to have instant access to it whenever I use my computer. I may write sequels, because it could be the beginning of a much larger story. At the end, it is rather clear that the protagonist, Michael Anderson, has decided to go off to the alien's planet (Ich Bien Stellars.) I think that the dialogue is priceless. Here's an excerpt:

The alien named Bob laughed. "You don't waste any time. I am from a planet far away. We-"

"What's the name of the planet?"

"What difference does it make? The name is in a language of which you know not a single word. Besides, names are so arbitrary. If you have to know, the name of my planet is 'Ich Bine Stellars.' My name isn't really Bob. That's just a name I am using for your convenience."

"Cool."

"We do come in peace, but you are lucky we even came at all."

"Yeah, I thought those short aliens with the big heads that abduct people would have been the ones to make an appearance."

The alien laughed again. This time it was with condescension. He stopped for a moment and then let out one final hysterical burst of laughter. His ears jingled back and forth while he did this. "Those dweebozoids!"

"Is that what they're called?"

"No, it's 1980s' slang. They are never going to make an appearance. Those aliens are voyeurs and collectors. Aside from watching and occasionally stealing a person for a few hours, they do very little. They are intergalactic perverts."

"How do you know 80s' slang, or even English for that matter?"

"Television. You broadcast that crap day after day for the whole universe to see and hear."

October 20, 1997

I'm happy because I now have a friend who doesn't make me hate myself. His name is Dean. I can be better!

All of my old friends kept me down. They discouraged me and allowed me to grow so complacent. I will be better! I will write bigger and better stories. I am a fiction writer!

October 21, 1997

Okay. That was too giddy. I spoke to my freshman composition professor today about my new ambition, and he suggested that I keep a regular journal. "You should read. That's a given, but many writers underestimate the value of a journal. Think of it as a warm-up exercise," Professor Grayson said. Between cool new friends and renewed commitment to this journal, I should be a stellar writer very soon.

From the Literary Exercises/Journal of Jed Haele

July 9, 2003

There's one week left until I need to distribute something releasable, but I am not going to write about that today, because I need to brainstorm. I get ideas from this journal when I write about my life, so here goes . . .

I didn't go to work today. My brother, Chester, filled in at the Midtown store that I manage, because he's on vacation from school and doesn't have a job. I don't mind giving the little bastard a chance to show off for the 'rents. The 'rents don't care because they're away. One's in Los Angeles. The other is visiting his/her family, or having an affair in Europe. Who knows? Mom might be the one in Europe, because I think she spends one month each summer abroad. That's right. However, in her condition, I am amazed she can still do it.

I renewed my driver's license this morning. Yes, I finally went for a new photo. Now I will look like myself. Bouncers will no longer squint when they try to match that eighteen-year-old with a goofy smile and blubbery corn-fed white cheeks up to the tanned and fabulously emaciated face they see today.

Simon's client's movie opened, and it's a hit. I read yesterday's ***Daily Variety*** over lunch in my apartment, and the final figures show that ***Sorority Road Trip*** did nearly twenty-four million over five days. The figure is impressive, since the July 4 weekend provided "high octane" competition. On the other hand, ***Dinosaur Attack 2*** was a relative disappointment, due to its mammoth $175-million budget. It made sixty-eight million over the five days, and now ***Dinosaur Attack 3*** may be a dubious prospect for the studio, according to Daily Variety.

Simon called me a few hours later and was ecstatic at first. He bragged about the weekday numbers and joked about the "failure" of the competition. In addition, he advised me that his film would get a sequel. "It'll be out next summer."

"That's great. Brooke must be stoked."

"Her role in SRT2: Crusin' will be MUCH larger."

"Pardon? What's that title?"

"SRT is an acronym for Sorority Road Trip. Get it? SRT2: Cruisin.' It'll be set on a cruise ship."

"Is that for real, Simon?"

"Yeah, why?" he asked, sincerely baffled by my question.

"A cruise is not a road trip. They are two different things."

"Well, I'm not a writer, so I don't care," he wheezed into the phone. He was hoarse from all of the calls he'd fielded in the last few days since the release of the film. Then, he started to cry. He was sad because he didn't have anybody else with which to celebrate, because "all my friends are still in school and it's a school night. I've been on IMBD all day reading the reviews. Not one review mentioned her. Not a single god-damned one!" He growled through more bitter tears.

He came over and blew me. That was cool, but I didn't appreciate it when he drank my booze from the bottle beforehand. Granted, his lips were on my cock a few minutes later, but still.

Janine called me later in the afternoon to ask about the chapter, because she's going away this weekend with her "friend." In other words, she's tired of waiting for me to finish the chapter and pay her . . . I have to cut this off. I promised at the outset that there would be no writing process ramblings today! I guess that means I can't describe the calls I got from two of my writing colleagues. Oh, well.

It's a weeknight, and I love to go out on weeknights, because the crowds at the clubs are smaller, and the music is not as loud.

What will happen? First, I get drunk. I drink vodka and Diet Coke. Then, I dance, and unbutton my fitted button-down shirt one button at a time to reveal my eight-pack abs. Soon, I'm dancing with a chick who has cleavage and long hair (I've got a bit of a hair fetish. The hair needs to be at least shoulder length. If it's too short, I stay limp. It's as simple as that.) I prick tease her and then depart. "Later, babe. I got to score," I say. It's a lie. I don't do drugs, but scoring drugs is a neat excuse to get away. Since I don't look unhealthy, chick #1 figures I'm only a recreational user, and she bops around to crappy remixes, waiting for me and my abs to return. Chick #2 will be different. Possibly, she'll have different colored hair or be aggressive and grab my ass.

Something will distinguish her, and once I have three somewhat different ones on the line, I sashay onto the dance floor, strut through the weekday crowd, and grab her soft pink hand.

I could also stay home and write, but Dean is game to hang with the str8's tonight and I always score when I bring my gay best friend along. Chicks dig that, even when I slip and call them chicks.

From the Journal of Dean

July 8, 2003

Two days' silence. I feel bad, especially when I read that shit where I tried to deconstruct the motivations for my prior career. No bullshit. It did it for the cash. I can't do that hypocritical lying thing.

It's a weekday. I'm tired and don't feel like writing.

July 9, 2003

Too tired again. Maybe on the weekend I'll make time and have something to say. I can't crap out a page about a mundane weekday. It's pointless. Besides, I'm on my way out. I'm meeting up with Jed at Eclectic tonight.

July 10, 2003

I have something to write about today. It's not about my day. It's old news.

I won $100,000 on a reality show called ***Fate*** last year. The premise of the show was confusing and neat, and I want to describe it.

There were ten contestants at the start. Each contestant was randomly assigned a fated rank from one to ten. We were not allowed to disclose our names to one another, and referred to each other solely by our fated numerical rank. For example, my initial fate was to finish in seventh place, so people called me Seven. Each week, the person fated to leave challenged this by participating in a competition. They targeted a person of a higher rank, and if they won, then the person of the higher rank would be forced to swap fates with them. If Ten targeted One, and won the challenge, then One would leave and Ten would be the new One. The participants broke into teams each week, which they chose among themselves. For example, Eight, Nine, and Ten teamed up in the first week and went against One through Seven in the competition. Seven players versus three may seem unfair, but they designed the challenges so that this didn't matter. The first challenge involved a quiz based upon a dossier about the ten contestants. Each person completed the quiz in isolation, and the team with the best average score won. My team averaged 76 percent and they averaged 72 percent. It was a timed competition, and we learned the results at the "Meet Your Fate Elimination Ceremony." Ten was eliminated, and One retained his rank.

In my game, Eight, Nine, and Ten bit the dust. Then, I teamed up with Five and Six. We targeted One, and beat the team of One, Two, Three, and Four at the challenge. I swapped fates with One, and he was eliminated. Six targeted Two the following week, and Five targeted Three the week after that. We succeeded at both challenges. Four was isolated. He competed by himself the following week and lost.

Thus, my alliance prevailed. I was the big winner, and have lived off my winnings ever since. The money is almost gone, but that was a fun once-in-a-lifetime ride.

(Later)

Okay. I should be honest. I wrote that description of the game out beforehand. I did drafts and made revisions. It was not spontaneous text. I revised it to be as clear and concise as possible.

I want to be a writer like Jed. However, I just don't see the point of crapping down the page without revising myself.

July 11, 2003

I'm so pathetic. I'm writing in my journal at 10:00 a.m. God! That's pathetic.

I did not pay my rent yet because my savings have run out, so I have to leave at the end of the week. In the words of my Russian landlord, who pounded her big-boned arm on my door far too early this morning, "Leave Sunday, or my boys vill chrow you out on the next Monday." I can't afford to pay, so I guess it's time to move back to Jed's place. I've lived with him from time to time, because he's like, you know, rich. He OWNS his two-bedroom apartment in Chelsea at the ripe old age of twenty-four. I guess there's lots of money to be made in sandwiches and subterranean online publishing of hackwork to taste and social skill–deprived college students with so much free time on their hands that they create message boards to discuss Jed's upcoming releases at every single stage. OK. I'm a little jealous.

However, he is a great friend who I know won't turn me away. I have to give him credit.

(Later)

"Hi!"

"Hey, Dean."

"Did you get hard-core action last night?"

"Nah. I left just after you."

"Aww."

"I'm busy this week. It's hard to relax. You know that."

"With it."

"Yes, it."

"Cool. Listen, I need a favor."

"Yeah . . . of what sort? I'm busy."

"To . . . stay, um . . ."

"Of course you can stay here."

"Thanks."

"I'm writing, so I can't help."

"Moving?"

"Yeah. Come by to get the key and move in while I'm at work tomorrow."

"Great! Thank you, so much."

"Bye."

I wanted to get all that dialogue down, because when I write fiction, I need good dialogue, so I am doing my best to listen to people and become aware of speech patterns. Jed suggested this when I told him that a paragraph-after-paragraph account of my day wasn't working for me.

Another problem is that I don't have any viable plot ideas. We talked about this on Sunday over lunch at the French bakery near his place. I don't remember the exact conversation, so I'm paraphrasing the dialogue. He started: "I get ideas from everywhere. I spoke to the guy who mangled his hand at Maran a few weeks ago. They had to cut it off."

"They couldn't . . ."

"Fix it? Nope. They must have chopped it off to prevent infection. Anyway, he still thinks I'm a monster. That's fabulous, because it's different. I'm thinking of myself as an observing destroyer and channeling those feelings into the text. The villain is a sphinx. It's oddly autobiographical, because it's a deranged take on my own experiences with him."

"But I thought autobiographical writing is a sign of inexperience."

"That's the thing. I'm a vessel . . ."

I can't transcribe any more of this shit. Jed is a nice guy, but he frequently takes himself way too seriously.

From the Literary Exercises/Journal of Jed Haele

July 10, 2003

Chester tended the store very well this week. I dropped in around 1:00 today. The line moved, the floor was clean, and somebody remembered to stock lids at the beverage stand. He gets an A. I delegated well. With that said, I'm halfway successful. Then, there's chapter two.

Chapter two starts with violence, but I cannot come up with any compelling "B" stories to kill time. Sean doesn't sleep well that evening, due to the fight he witnessed, but I got nowhere writing about how he's pissed off about being tired the next day.

I called some of my friends for ideas. Makiko suggested that I focus on Sean's reaction to the violence. Yost expressed additional skepticism about the narrative perspective. His suggestion was that I "swap protagonists at some point so we get the P.O.V. of Julian. Then, you can debunk Sean's beliefs to a certain extent." That notion intrigues me, but I don't want to end up with another ***Untitled***, i.e., a novel that fails due to a risky story structure. Simon thinks I can't do the "closet case" thing subtly, so I should make him openly gay if he is in fact gay. Janine said she'd fix whatever I gave her, so I went back to the drawing board relaxed. Janine fixes it. That's my writing mantra.

From the Journal of Janine

July 13, 2003

Besides waiting for Jed's chapter (I expect it tomorrow or the day after), I've been trying to figure out my schedule next semester. Every class I want is closed, and I don't want to nag my dean or wait on line until August. Next year I won't have to worry about such things.

Of course, I won't have the summer off, unless Jed suddenly becomes much more productive and he can pay me as if I was his assistant. I don't want a real job. I don't want to be a dime-a-dozen employee in my "chosen" profession. Ugh. Soon enough, I'll have to start throwing resumes against the wall to see if any stick. It's not really ambition anymore, is it? It's all about settling, and that is so patronizing.

I guess I'm down because the weekend turned to shit. Darwin is my new boyfriend. He might be gay, but it's a tough call. It's usually obvious, but closet cases are increasingly adept at sending signals to throw me off. He noticed most of the attractive women who passed our table at Banyon's Steakhouse last night and subtly eyed them. However, he sporadically checked out the guys, when he thought I wasn't looking.

Maybe he's bisexual. Who knows? Who cares? He didn't call me today. That means he's either a straight asshole, or a gay pretending to be a straight asshole. I'm not sure which scenario is worse!

The Sunday newspaper has not perked me up at all. There's a blurb in one about this decomposing lady who was found Friday on the side of a highway in Pennsylvania, with a note in her pocked that read, "I wanted to go home." They haven't identified her yet, because her wallet was stolen.

She rotted there for at least a week and "most of her internal organs were eaten by passing scavengers." That's a pleasant note on which to end this grim entry.

July 14, 2003

I don't want to type anymore. Chapter two was absolutely horrible. He gave me thirty-five pages of drivel, and within fourteen hours, I turned it into a fair twelve-page continuation of the initial chapter. Here's some of it:

When I escaped the bus, the thin man stood up and stared at me through the window with his gray eyes as it blasted ahead.

And I was alone, worried that there was too little night left for me to replenish my energy with sleep. I walked the block to my apartment, and my mind flashed rapidly cutting images of that thin and finely dressed observer, who may have been wearing a wig over his presumably bald head. These images haunted me when I tried to fall asleep minutes later on my silky soft mattress. I did not sleep at all that night.

I cut all the violence, because it was too silly. The pages he gave me resembled a body ravaged with metastic cancer. Once you cut all the pounds of malignancy away, what remains is still dying.

Only the flashback to Sean's days of deprogramming reminded me of Jed's talent. Sean's exhaustion the next day reminds him of when an exiter deprogrammed him from an esoteric religious cult. Said cult tracked a line of divinity back hundreds of years through an eclectic combination of historical figures from across the globe. Of course, that line ended with the charismatic leader, who was a second cousin of a certain contemporary Hollywood superstar.

When I'm forced to wade through endless pages of clumsily constructed fight scenes, it's easy to forget that he is a talent. He successfully established a history of mental instability for his character through the back-story and cleverly linked it to current events in his character's life. The reader understands that Sean can lose it.

Regardless, it is not working. He developed scant effective secondary stories in the new chapter. In addition, the fight scene will be missed later on, because the first one will not exist in the text for comparison and contrast. Unfortunately, it had to go. Its inclusion would have done far more harm, and he knows it. It was poorly written and unintentionally funny.

From the Journal of Jed Haele

May 3, 2001

Graduation is two weeks away. I just finished my last final exam ever. That Investment Finance Seminar was a bitch for most of the semester, but the final exam was unexpectedly straightforward.

Beatrice had her last final yesterday and is quite sour. She doesn't have a job yet and resents me because my dad offered me a job. I intend to accept his offer to manage one of his restaurants, so her rage will only grow. I'm sure of it.

May 9, 2001

I remember so little of the last week that I'm convinced that I have traveled in time. I binge drank that much!

I'm so miserable, and drank so much that I think I aged five years. I am dreading this nine-to-five bullshit so much that I think I may bail. I don't want to do it. It's as simple as that.

Okay, enough for now. I need to go puke. I'm so fucked up today.

May 11, 2001

Beatrice and I had a violent fight. Let's break it down.

She showed up at my house uninvited. She was in a rotten mood from her hopeless job search and wanted to have another conversation about nepotism.

"It's a fucking sandwich shop in Midtown! Jesus!" I yelled. "What is your problem?"

She shook her head so violently I thought she was going to give herself whiplash. "Don't you throw that bullshit angle at me. What's next? Are you going to whine about how Daddy made you work every summer when you were a teenager?"

"Yes! Why the fuck not! Yeah! You should construe that as me working my way up, babe! Nobody ever forced you to do anything, and now you're paying the price for it."

Enough of this! I am so sick of her.

May 24, 2001

The dark night of my soul begins tomorrow when I report to Sterling Subs for duty. I've been too depressed to write lately and will likely continue to be for a long time. This sucks.

From the Literary Exercises/Journal of Jed Haele

December 1, 2001

I am ready for this. Okay! Let's go!

This is my new "journal." I've kept a journal for years, but I've decided that I need to approach it in a different manner, because I am a novelist now. This new "journal" will have multiple functions. It remains a document of my life and times, but will also serve as a forum for me to brainstorm about writing, as well as a "behind the scenes" record of my creative process. I will also maintain a writer's "junk yard," but I will do my best to keep that material separate from this journal.

Why am I a novelist? I just re-read the closing entries of my last journal, and they sum it up rather well. I need to write in order to cope with/escape the banality of real life.

Once I adjusted to the soul-killing reality of nine-to-five last summer, I decided that the only way I could remain human was to revisit my interest in writing fiction. It has entailed a great deal of work to get to this point, but I had to take the leap.

The first step was a distribution plan. As a writer with no agent, completed text, or time and interest in pounding the pavement, I chose to use the Internet. In this area, my friend Simon was quite helpful. I created my web site (jedhaele.com) with his assistance. There are message boards, a biography of myself, a plot summary for the novel, and an option to pre-order the novel, which will be ready on April 23, 2002. The web site has received 2917 hits so far. In addition, I have sold eighteen copies of my unwritten novel to date.

Shelby will be the title of my first novel. The title, genre, and plot were critical choices. In order to develop my genre and plot, I reviewed all of the short stories and poetry that I wrote in college. I decided that a thriller, with elements of horror would be a solid mélange of genres. The plot is in flux now, but I do have a general idea and that is sufficient for the website right now.

Another element was marketing. Simon assisted me in this area as well. His first suggestion was good old-fashioned flyers. I will distribute them at the local colleges beginning in January. In addition, he suggested that I log hours in appropriately themed chat rooms, and direct these people to the website. This will function as grassroots marketing. In addition, I will expand the website as the text comes together. This should entice visitors to return and tell their friends to come too.

Finally, I needed a typist, because I hate typing. I intend to write the novel in longhand and submit it to a typist a few chapters at a time. I went back to my school and tracked down Professor Grayson in October. I advised him of my needs, and he recommended a sophomore named Janine. "She's sharp, energetic, and hungry. You'll love her." He gave her my number, and she called me over Thanksgiving weekend. We negotiated a price per page deal.

Now, I must write ***Shelby***.

From the Literary Exercises/Journal of Jed Haele

July 14, 2003

The unkindest and most audacious cut was not a slap in the face. Janine cut the fight, and I was not surprised because I knew she would. Consequently, there's only a slight indication that Sean thinks that Julian is evil. The prior cult membership thing and small hints at Julian's psychic abilities allow the chapter to slump along with some element of novelty. It's now a twelve-page Word document on a floppy disk that contains 4993 words.

I just sent it out, two days early, as per Simon's suggestion. I called him, and once he heard that it was finished, he said, "Dear God! Why haven't you sent it out yet? There's no more bullish sign than moving up a release date." Granted, the original plan would have had the chapter come out last Friday, but still.

From the Journal of Justin Simonds

July 14, 2003

Today I got a most unexpected treat. Jed Haele distributed the second chapter of his latest two days early. I got home from work and checked my e-mail. The subject line read, "Good things come to those who cannot wait . . ." I clicked, downloaded, printed, and read it.

I wish he'd give the damn thing a title so I'd have a better sense of where the novel is headed. So far, I don't understand what I'm paying for. It's his most conservative work yet, and he's edited it to within an inch of its life. It's choppy, but I don't think the excised material would have helped, or been interesting enough to make it worth the time to read. The most audacious element so far is the abrupt start of the second chapter. It speeds past the fight which chapter one's conclusion seemed to promise. In some sort of off-kilter way it works, but I expect a real treat when I read Jed Haele. I want to have fun. The twenty-seven pages he has released so far are joyless.

In other news, I'm on vacation this week. It's great. Constance is off too, because her summer session just ended. I'm glad Shane introduced us to one another. She may be a prudish academic, but damn! Once she knocks back a few bottles of beer, the lady is fun.

That reminds me. I haven't seen Shane for weeks. Every time I call him, he makes an excuse about how he has to get "out of town" for the weekend. It's weird. I asked Constance about him the other day, and all she said was, "He did what he had to do with Hunter, and I think he's depressed." Oh, well. It's summertime. I can't waste my time waiting for him. That's all for now.

Form the Journal of Sharisse

July 15, 2003

Clea is jonesing on the stairs listening to a Bad Company CD on her boom box. I'm waiting for the phone to ring. Cecil is supposed to call when he's ready for me. He's a shady dealer. He invites certain clients to his pad, whilst the others must meet him at any random isolated and creepy location he chooses: outside a porn shop in Brooklyn, in an alley about a block away from a Gray's Papaya stand, a park known by the locals as Needle Park, in a nightclub bathroom, etc.

To be honest, I'm down on the junk, because I think Hunter is dead. I hope that she isn't, but she probably is. The last time we spoke was on her birthday.

That was hell on earth. She didn't show up for the party at my house. I called her, and she spoke unintelligibly in syllables and grunts. She hurled over the phone, into the receiver, and the line died!

Clea, Marvin, and Tim sighed. "I'm going, mother fuckers." I went to her apartment, but . . . Cecil called! Yes! Yes! Yes! Clea just sprung up from the stairs and did a little dance! I'll write more eventually.

From the Literary Exercises/Journal of Jed Haele

July 18, 2003

Simon is so clever. The early release had a positive impact. I now have more than 2000 subscribers. Yes, there has been a bump in subscribers for an incomplete book, which has yet to provide much of a thrill.

Regardless, people seem to like the new chapter. I finally perused the message boards, and the fans are mildly amused, but they are also quite anxious for the third chapter, which is currently scheduled for release on July 30. I think that they expect more of the freaky stuff and action. With that said, I have a second chance at drafting a competent fight sequence. I need to deliver it. I know that their patience (i.e., the "mild amusement" displayed on the message boards) is based more on my track record than the first two chapters.

I understand what went wrong last time, and I will learn from my mistakes. My choice of combatants was overly broad and silly. A public bus was an unlikely setting for a grisly fight. In addition, Julian should not have awkwardly stood there and stared at them while they fought. It was too obvious, and I would have shot my wad by including it.

The reader and the protagonist (i.e., Sean) do not yet fully realize that Julian plays some role in the conflicts. He's just a weird guy, who happens to be there. The second encounter will incite his deja vu and subsequent madness.

The setting for the fight is crucial. Public transportation or any crowded environment just won't work. Rather, I need isolation and coincidence, because this is the point where the paranoia begins.

July 19, 2003

Believe it or not, I got another message from Shane. He wanted to talk more, and to my surprise, he gave me his telephone number. I invited him to come over for tea and petit fours tomorrow afternoon.

In retrospect, I wish I didn't invite him, and give him my home address. He was overly confident at the restaurant when he showed off the stub where his hand used to be. Then, he boldly gave me his home phone number in the e-mail today. That's strange, because he was so paranoid before.

July 20, 2003

He shifted on my black leather sofa, as if he had hemorrhoids or a twisted ball sack. He kept "the stump" in his pants pocket. I sat in front of my desk by the window, with my back to the computer. "I'm not doing anything at the moment, Shane. You can relax," I said soberly.

He scoffed. "I know you aren't. I can tell now."

I leaned forward and smirked. "Really?" His eyelid twitched, and he grinned uneasily. I tried to deepen my voice. "You could be in danger, and what would you do?" I asked.

He scoffed again. "I know what you do, and I've told people about it. If I die, you will be exposed." He jerked his wrist around some more and crudely adjusted something in his pocket. "Why don't you explain it? The plan?"

"What do you think it is?"

"You and your kind will remain in the shadows, forcing your will upon strangers. You will cause escalating violence, but the secrecy will protect you from any consequences. And . . ." He paused and bugged his eyes out.

"What?" I asked.

"And it will end. Society will disintegrate."

"Why would I do that?"

"Because you can. Your kind has no morals. You are corrupt!" He pulled the "stump" out of his pocket.

"So you think you are safe now, right? With your little cavalry of people who know about me." He nodded. "Well, if that's the case then why are you here?"

"Empathy."

"Empathy?"

"You don't understand?"

"Oh, I do, Shane. I really do. You have empathy for all these people who will suffer because of my powers. You feel sorry for their pain, injuries, and death, and you want to do something about it. I get it. You're such a hero." I enjoyed deconstructing this new wrinkle in the moment, but immediately decided it wasn't useful for my book. I considered bringing in the angle he brought up in the restaurant about wishing he had the power to save people, but that just shut him off when I prodded it last time. I decided to switch gears. "What are you going to do about us? My kind?"

"I don't know." He paused. "I do know that you are a Destroyer, and there are others like you. I will find a way to expose you."

"Are you willing to die? You said it yourself. If I kill you, then I will be exposed to the whole wide world." He stared at me speechless, but not afraid. He was pondering. "Are you willing to take your empathy to the next level and be a casualty? You could save so many people." I paused to give him time to think it through and give me more.

"I'm not ready."

"No?"

"I'm not ready to die."

"So you're a coward?" I said sternly. "A pathetic coward who's fucking with the wrong person."

He leaned forward in my sofa. "No, I am calculating, and I when I am done figuring out what I need to do, you will be the first to find out. Please rest assured of that, Destroyer!" That's a response to what I said? He needs to calculate? I suppose this dearth of efficiency and confidence could help me pad out the book. On the other hand, I could develop this from the perspective of cautious strategizing by the protagonist, i.e., patience is a virtue for him. The incongruence of forethought and crazy seems like a good idea actually.

"In the meantime then you have nothing to worry about."

"Yes," he said confidently. "I already told you. My friends know about you."

I cackled as maniacally as I could. ***I can destroy you with three words,*** I thought, and then said, "Nobody believes you."

His face turned red, and both of his eyelids pulsed. "Your friends?" I scoffed. "These people who you told." I cackled some more and stared at him. "Oh, golly. I'm sure that they were very receptive to all this." I flashed a smug grin.

"They did get . . ." he trailed off.

"Oh, I am sure that they did!" I nodded and went for the jugular. "You are so close. I could kill you without getting out of this chair!" I let out some more guffaws, and he abruptly left.

Thank you, Shane! I'm through with him, because I have extracted enough material from him about his delusions, and his perspective on my "villainy." That's the first half of the book. Now, I need to construct a model for the redemptive side of the character that I will develop in the second half. That character will be pure fiction.

(Later)

The fight takes place at night. Sean's boss forces him to work overtime again. He enters the restroom, and two coworkers are calmly conversing at their respective urinals. Julian walks in, and they fight to the death. It's a bathroom, so every clang and crash of bones on the walls and floor echoes. Sean is a mess of tics and twitches, while Julian is the model of icy cool serenity and composure. He slinks away.

It takes Sean a minute to add two and two together. He tries to catch Julian, but he's gone. He talks to his friends about it the next day, and they think he's crazy. They weren't there and didn't absorb the urgency of the situation first hand. The restroom combatants are the least of Sean's concern, because he fixates on Julian. He needs to understand Julian. However, his friends are more concerned with their injured coworkers than the mysterious stranger. This frustrates Sean greatly.

Sean wishes to solve the puzzle and figure out how to unmask Julian. He doesn't know Julian's name, so he calls him "The Sphinx."

From the Journal of Janine

July 24, 2003

There's a back-story now, and a convincing spiral into madness. I don't know if Jed's plan for redemption for his protagonist will work, but Jed's new chapter is the fastest eighteen pages I ever read or typed. It's absolutely fabulous. I didn't change a word, for the first time ever.

He called me at like six this morning and left a message for me to come over today to get the pages. I showed up at ten, and he had them wrapped in the manila envelope all ready for me. He was effusively happy. He didn't say much, but high-fived me before he went to his kitchen to get me a snack. There was a spring in his step. I'd never actually seen that cliché in reality, and it was actually somewhat scary. His gams bounced up as if they were weightless.

It's better because this chapter has a structure and, to an extent, applies one retroactively to the prior two. The three chapters could stand on their own as accounts of Sean's paranoia. The opening of chapter three reiterates the character's desire for a regular regimen. Work demands interrupt it, and this throws him off balance again. Then, there's a fight in the bathroom. ***The "bad guy"*** (a.k.a. ***"The Sphinx"***) is there, and Sean decides that he telepathically initiated the conflict. The next day, Sean explains this theory to his disbelieving friends. The chapter ends with him ever-so-cautiously walking home from work, terrified that ***"The Sphinx"*** will appear in every ***"alley and dark street he passes."*** It's a brilliant conclusion. Apparently, he's afraid of the bus, because that's where he first saw ***"The Sphinx."***

I just wish the cult thing from chapter two would come back, because that was a bewitching twist. I think Jed is researching that, because there was a book about David Koresh on his coffee table today.

From the Journal of Justin Simonds

July 26, 2003

Holy fucking shit!

A couple of weeks ago, Shane told me an absurd story, and I laughed it off. I attributed it to his overactive imagination. Then I read the latest chapter of Jed's new novel this afternoon, and it takes a turn that mimics Shane's story. I called Constance and explained the situation to her.

"How close is it?" she asked.

"It's obvious."

"How much do you know about this writer?" she asked, growing more concerned. I explained to her that he's an underground writer who has an online readership. "Underground?"

"Yes. Is that important?"

"Well, yeah!" She scoffed. "He could be anybody."

"I hope you're not suggesting that . . ."

"Did Shane ever see Zeke again, after that . . . train thing?"

"No?" He likely wouldn't have said anything, since we didn't take him seriously and rolled our eyes back more each time he mentioned it. "I think I asked him about it once, but . . . it's not true."

"I need to read it."

I forwarded the chapter to her. I'm waiting for her to come over. I thought it would be a good idea to send the chapter to Shane also, but she told me to hold off until we see him.

July 27, 2003

When she arrived, I knew she agreed with me. Her eyes were red. She probably cried on the train. Constance is a coldly logical person and I'm sure that this enigma devastated her. "We can't do anything," she said, slumping down onto my couch. "You haven't seen Shane lately, have you?"

"I thought he was supposed to move to California, but I rang him a few times and he was still there."

"You spoke to him?"

"No, but I got the machine. The message is still the same. It's his."

She lowered her head, fingered the arch of her nose, and looked down at her boots.

"Maybe Shane is Jed Haele?" I suggested.

She released her hand from her nose and shook her head. "That'd be too simple, and isn't plausible. Shane is Shane, but this writer? Jed Haele? He's telling a story that's too close to life."

"What about the book Shane is always writing in?"

"No. That's a journal." Then, a light bulb went on in her mind. She popped her head up. "I know where he keeps them. Remember that day when we took him to the beach and Hunter and Sharisse came over?" I nodded. "I got bored. I snooped around his room and found them."

"Them?"

"The journals! He has at least a dozen of them in a box on the shelf high up in his closet. He writes so much that I'm sure he's on another book by now."

We took the local train to Elmhurst. When we got to the station, I bolted up the stairs two or three steps at a time. Constance followed me closely at a surprisingly rapid pace. Once we reached the open air, it was fully dark. She slipped on a pair of sunglasses and covered her shoulder-length blond hair with a fitted black cap.

"Is that necessary?" I asked. She grunted and walked faster. "How do you break into an apartment?" I asked slyly.

She laughed. "That's a good one. I didn't think about that."

"If he's home, we can just invite ourselves in, and you can sneak into his room while I catch up with him," I suggested. "If not?"

"What do you think? Are you up for it?" she asked.

"I would rather not."

"Then we won't."

When we reached his building, we saw that his name was scratched off the block next to the buzzer. I rang it repeatedly, but got no response. We looked at each other.

"But he's still in New York," she said. "You said that you got his machine last week. This doesn't make any sense."

It didn't, so we went back to my place and did a search on the Internet for Jed Haele. Constance couldn't believe that I had never done this before. I reminded her that I have better things to do than sit at home all day researching subterranean novelists. There were a few fan sites, but they had no pictures. Most had recent updates in response to the "kick-ass" new chapter. There was a blurb about him in a ***Wired*** article and a small photo, but we couldn't tell what he looked like because he was wearing sunglasses and the photo was tinted dark.

Once we reached the fourth page of search results, she remarked, "This is pointless. Is there any way to contact Jed Haele? That'd be the easiest . . ." I shook my head. "There has to be a way. It might help him," she added.

I decided to act against her wishes at this point, but kept it from her. It is only fair that he know, as the events depicted in the novel may be a variation upon real-life incidents. After she left, I forwarded the chapter to Shane.

From the Literary Exercises/Journal of Jed Haele

July 27, 2003

I'm writing chapter four right now, because it's foolish to resist the momentum. Sean will encounter Julian in a public spot and expect a fight to break out. At this point, Julian will toy with him. I'm drawing from the conversation I had with Shane the other day.

There will be no fight. Instead, Julian will lure Sean into a more secluded spot and goad him. Sean will slap Julian across the face. This blow will cause a small cut on Julian's cheek, and he will bleed chalk white blood. This cliffhanger ending will lay the groundwork for the reveal that Julian is an alien. It will indicate to the reader that Julian is some sort of "other."

July 28

Quite unexpectedly, I had another conversation with Shane over the phone, and most unfortunately, the cat is now out of the bag. It would be boring to transcribe the entire conversation, because he took forever to make his point. Finally, he just asked, "What's the deal? You're a writer, in addition to a telepathic who incites violence in people?"

I certainly didn't anticipate this. Is he one of my readers? I finally decided that this was ridiculous. Since I no longer needed to observe his insanity for material, I decided to pull off the mask once and for all. "I'm not a killer. Those were just coincidences. I've been using your delusions to serve as material for the book I'm writing. I am a novelist. I didn't trigger any violence."

He refused to acknowledge my confession. Rather, he interpreted it as a Byzantine trick. "Your wickedness will not stand." His speech was more forceful now. "You try to deny it." He scoffed. "Once you're exposed and . . . open for the world to see, everybody will understand what you are."

He hung up and I slammed my receiver. Dean drowsily popped up on the couch. "Fuck, man," he whined.

"Sorry?"

"You woke me up . . . What was that?"

"Shane," I said quietly, hoping he wouldn't hear.

He released a throaty giggle. "Fucking Shane. I thought you were done with him."

"So did I," I said grimly. I think I speak to Shane more than I do with some of my friends these days.

I've decided that the first three-week break will be between the chapter I released on Friday and the next one. August 15 is my target now. That gives me time to think about the reality that currently haunts my fiction.

From the Journal of Justin Simonds

July 31, 2003

I got an e-mail from Shane today. The text was as follows:

I enjoyed being friends with you very much, but I must finally move away now. I will leave for San Diego next week and buy an apartment. Ever since my brother died, it's felt like every door has shut itself in my face, leaving me in darkness. I need to get as far away as possible. I will e-mail you the address, but I will understand if you need to move on.

I read that little story. I didn't enjoy it at all.

I'm surprised. I thought that the chapter would have offended him more. Whatever! I still don't buy Shane's story, and I won't really miss him. He's been such a drag lately.

From the Journal of Dean

August 1, 2003

I've lived with Jed for a few weeks, and I haven't written. It's silly to apologize, but I should. If I had made entries over the last few days, it would be easier to describe what's strange.

The last few days have been especially weird. In full view of Jed, I screwed Simon on the black leather sofa yesterday. It did not surprise me that he wanted to watch, but as I thrusted into Simon, he pulled out his tape recorder. It was kinky. He stared at us as if we were his science project. I thrusted really hard toward the end, and Simon screamed.

Incidentally, Simon is hot, and his thighs are awesome. I never noticed this before, but he was wearing a nice pair of acid washed jeans, and they emphasized his shapely thighs. Nothing turns me on more than a muscular set of thighs in the right pair of jeans.

Jed's voyeurism is just one component of his recent funky vibe. He's supposed to be working on the fourth chapter of his book, but he changes the topic whenever I bring it up. He left a very rough draft on the coffee table recently. I looked it over, and it did not read well at all. He says he'll finish it in one long sleepless stretch when the release date is "more imminent." I think he's afraid of finishing the chapter because of his increasingly bizarre interactions with this freak named Shane Lasch.

I don't want to tell the entire story. In short, Shane has delusions and Jed used them as the backbone for his current novel. The problem is that Shane is increasingly adamant about his beliefs and Jed is now spooked.

From the Literary Exercises/Journal of Jed Haele

July 30, 2003

I went back to work today (I'm writing this at work), because I think one of the 'rents is due back this week. I think it's Dad, and he's returning from a month on the Riviera. Yeah. That makes sense. He goes to Europe, and Mom could be anywhere. She usually travels for the entire month of July. I am amazed that she can still do it in her condition. Chester fucked up the orders, so this week's shipment was off—too much turkey and too many veggie patties, but not enough ham. Once I got through covering my ass, I ripped him a new one over the phone and watered down a Diet Coke with some vodka. I get to go home soon.

(Later)

Dean was out, of course. He perused the draft of chapter four that I laid out of the coffee table and left the following comments on Post-Its: "Short

Chapter, huh?" "Yet still tan human skin. How does that work?" "What if Sean didn't hit him hard enough to make him bleed?"

Fucking amateur! He thinks he can second-guess me and that I will let him. I know that he has never spent an evening sweating to make it fucking work on the page. At least Janine takes what I give her, works like a dog with no notice, and makes it as golden as it can be. At least Simon knows how to market intellectual property. At least my colleagues give constructive and educated advice. Dean has never read a book. Dean has got brass balls if he thinks he can barge in and comment upon my process.

No! He is the colorful character who drifts in and out of MY books. I observe him for raw material. I scan his clothes labels to see what designers are hot. I tape him when he doesn't know it in order to get dialogue samples.

Dean oversteps a big fucking boundary when he grills me about "the writing." If he nags me one more time for quick tips, I will never buy him a designer shirt ever again! He can't write, and it insults me that he aspires to accomplish what I've worked at for years without a fraction of the struggle and effort and pain and failure.

July 31, 2003

I was mean yesterday. That's what great about a journal. You can be mean, and there are no consequences.

There's this apparent pervert producer in Bulgaria who saw Simon's fat-assed client in ***Sorority Road Trip*** and wants to cast her in a lead role. Simon's scared because he doesn't want to go to Bulgaria and visit the guy. We found a photo of him on the Web this afternoon after work. He is bald, with acne and a creepy leering grin. "It's the yellow leather pants she wore in the scene where the camera lingered on her ass while she walked. Her ass!" Simon groaned. "He just wants to fuck her, and then he'll blow us off."

"Don't go."

"But it's a lead!" he pleaded, blissfully unconcerned with his flip-flop.

"Go!"

He rummaged his hands through his freshly cut and dyed dark hair and moaned, and I wondered if this was leading up to some sort of sex. Dean watched us from the couch and made a crude gesture. Simon smiled weakly and headed over to the couch. I watched what followed and discreetly taped the audio with my tape recorder. When I get a chance, I will transcribe the whole thing.

Part 3
The New Adjective

From the Journal of Jed Haele

August 5, 2003

I don't know how to write today. That's an odd statement to come from a writer who has thousands of eager readers anxiously awaiting the next chapter in his episodic new novel.

Fortunately, I am done with that chapter. Janine will slaughter it, as she must, and I have scheduled its release for next Friday. Then, then there will be a much harsher reality to consider. I no longer know how to write my novel.

The new novel was vaguely based on real world people (Shane Lasch and I), but that can no longer be the case, because that "reality" is now fundamentally changed.

Shane Lasch "infiltrated" my apartment yesterday afternoon. My neighbor subsequently indicated that she heard someone enter my apartment around noon. She assumed that it was me or a friend like Janine. He rummaged through the drawers and cabinets for hours in search of any evidence that I was the "lecherous demon responsible for many telepathic crimes." He successfully made a mess, but uncovered no evidence, of course.

Absent this evidence, he proceeded to the second part of his plan. He dragged my writing chair away from the computer, parked himself by my front door, and waited for me to come home.

While he waited, he composed an extended note on one of my legal pads. His "Statement of Fact," which was based upon his observations at our prior encounters, as well as at least two hours of unlimited search privileges of my apartment, indicated that he would not accept that I was just a successful fiction writer. Rather, he only believed in the Jed Haele that existed in his mind and decided that the writing was a cover. I was "The Destroyer."

His plan for revenge/heroism was twofold. He attached a pair of heated clamps to the inside door handle. "You shall briefly suffer before I execute you." In addition, he held a loaded pistol in his remaining hand.

At 4:30, the key went into the lock and the hand grasped the knob with a sizzle. According to my neighbor, there was a "hideous" yelp. Most appropriately, Shane did not even wait for the door to open so he could see a face. He shot the first bullet at chest level and sprayed the rest at skull height. The dying man slowly slid to the ground. The blood leaked out from his chest onto the door, and then his shoulders and hair brushed it down in jutty waves.

On his way out, Shane pulled at the blood-soaked dark hair to see that he just killed Dean instead of me. He must have gripped really hard, because the clump of hair that he snagged remained erect once he let go. Then, he disappeared.

August 6, 2003

It's a sad and sorry sight when you find yourself describing your failed assassin to the detectives as a "one-armed man." I realized that I got it wrong, since it's more accurate to call him a one-and-a-half-armed man.

The two detectives asked me an endless series of questions. One really frightened me. "Do you have any reason to believe that the assailant has infiltrated your home before?" The grim one grumbled, barely comprehensible. I invited Shane over once, but it never occurred to me that this was a hobby of his. The detective scratched his scaly bald scalp. "Well, sir?" he asked more forcefully. I shrugged my shoulders. The other detective, who was only slightly more upbeat, asked, "What about the slip of paper?"

"The slip?" I croaked. Shane had taped a piece of paper to Dean's back with a single typewritten line on it: "There is only one ending for your book." Obviously, that means death. "In my, um, literary opinion," I bullshitted, "that isn't a threat." Both of them scribbled onto their little pads now. Eventually, they left. On their way out, the grim one concluded, "It might be a good idea to stay elsewhere until we, um . . ."

"Find him," the other added. He smiled weakly.

(Later)

I refuse to run away and hide, so I booby-trapped my apartment. I took all of my serving platters and covered the bottom of them with duct tape with the sticky side facing up. Then, I placed slender one-and-a-half–inch nails over the tape. As luck would have it, I have four platters, and four windows! If he took that route, his fucking feet would be eviscerated. The long nails would protrude up through the shoe such that it would be more painful to take his foot out than to leave it in. Of course, leaving it in would entail more pain than childbirth. I also have a bottle of mace, among other weapons (which I will get too) nearby me while I sleep. If he goes this route, I will spray him in the eyes while he's incapacitated on the floor. Let's see? That's two limbs down, and a most important sense (i.e., sight), as well. That's the lucky scenario. If he's unlucky, then he will try the front door. If Shane returns to my apartment looking to finish the job, he will face an ending straight out of one of my novels!

I called Janine and described all of this to her. "Wow!" she said.

"I know! If only I could write as well." I paused, and she sighed. "Oh, yeah, that. Actually, I nearly finished my draft before the murder . . ."

"Are you sure that you're all right?" she asked. We did talk about Dean at the beginning of the conversation, but I rushed her off the subject, as this was primarily a business call. I really did not want to talk about it.

"I told you, Janine. I'll get through it. We'll delay it a bit. You'll have it by the fourteenth, and I want to release it on the twenty-ninth. That gives you two full weeks. Okay?"

"That works fine for me," she said.

I impulsively decided to delay chapter four from August 15 to August 29 while we spoke, because I may alter it radically. I need to think about this.
(Later)

I finally read yesterday's papers. I made page twelve of one tabloid ("A Haele-ish Scene!" the headline read.), and page twenty-three with a four-paragraph blurb in another. The former featured the standard publicity photo: Me, naked with sunglasses, with a laptop on my lap. It's from my ***Wired*** magazine blurb. Beside that photo was my worst nightmare: A photograph of my apartment building, with a caption that mentions my street address.

When I saw this, I immediately looked out my window. The street was empty. I sighed. On the one hand, I was pleased that there were no obsessed fans lurking below. On the other, one or two of them would have massaged my ego a bit.
(Shortly afterward)

What else can I do, but write? Except, I can't. I can't write that book now. Nevertheless, I have to. They all paid thirty dollars. I just checked. My list of subscribers for this new book has grown by over four hundred since the release of the well-received third chapter. That's twelve thousand dollars.

When I call Simon, he'll curtly offer his condolences. The only way I will keep him on the line is to tell him the good news about the subscribers.

"Fantastic! Fabulous!" he'll say, with his standard vapid intonation.

"A silver lining?" I'll add, fully aware that the sarcasm will go over his head.

"Exactly, Jed. You get it now. That's great!" he'll say.

This speculative conversation scares me. Do I dare to see how far it would go? If I actually called Simon, would my cynicism about him prove true?

(Later)

I have decided to pull the plug. I just disabled the subscription section of the website for the new book. The prospective new subscribers can do whatever the hell they want. If they know a subscriber and obtain a pirated text, then more power to them. They'll have a four-chapter novel.

It is fair. Surely, my subscribers will manage to barter themselves into the black and beyond with the new book. They will get the final chapter on August 29, and it will mark the end of my writing career.

Janine won't be happy. Neither will my writing buddies. Their consensus will be a chorus: "He had the career we all wanted to have and threw it way 'cause of some dead fag!" Simon won't find me interesting anymore either, for similar reasons. I won't satiate his vampire-like thirst for celebrity anymore.

August 7, 2003

I am a bad person. I can't pretend that I didn't trash Dean in here just days before he died.

(Later)

I did not leave my apartment again today. I sat at my computer and stared out the window for a two-hour stretch. Am I having a nervous breakdown?

August 8, 2003

I made a strange choice today. Instead of going to Dean's funeral, I watched all of the tapes of his reality series. I prepared my lunch of Eggs Colby around noon and started the first tape.

By the fourth episode, he is depressed because he expects to lose. Then, he turns it all around and wins.

August 9, 2003

I tried to do it. I tried to go out there and do what I do. I moussed my hair and slipped into the low-riding black slacks that make my ass look irresistible. I considered going shirtless. It is summer, after all! My abs did look great in the mirror, but I ultimately decided that I was too pale to pull that look off. I grabbed a red silk shirt from my closet.

I bit my nails for the first time in years on the train. I always feel empty on the train rides to the village, but tonight I also felt corrupt. I got out at West Fourth, and my vision was blurry.

I went to a new bar and only drank vodka straight. A few dim bulbs winked at me. One had too-big tits. Another had too-small tits. The third one's tits were just right, and she had pretty green eyes.

She far too abruptly stripped when we got to my apartment and turned out to be much fatter than I expected. My radar was so off. Usually I can detect it when a fatty poses and dresses to appear thinner. In addition, she was boring. Absent the bar's loud music, my silent apartment and my moderate buzz amplified her weak conversation skills. "I do want to have sex with you, Jed. I really do," she said in a catatonic drone. Her desperation irritated me. ***Why is this fucking person in my apartment***, I thought.

At least I didn't fuck her. That is such a relief. I cooed into her ear that she was "wonderful and worthwhile," while I gave her a back massage.

She's smoking in my bed now. I'm usually not a fan of secondhand smoke. I quit in 2000 and generally find it odious, but it is oddly appropriate tonight.

August 10, 2003

Damn! That bitch took forever to leave. Then Simon called.

"Hey, Simon."

"How was your weekend?"

"Um, it was," I huffed.

"The chapter?" He never beats around the bush.

"Oh, God. You didn't hear about it, did you?"

"No. What happened?"

"Dean's dead."

"So?" He scoffed.

"Shane Lasch killed him."

I imagined him bobbing his head and staring at a wall enraged. "Uh-huh."

"He fucked you. On my couch."

"Oh, that Dean. I'm sorry. He was fun."

"Shane shot him in the head and chest."

"Yikes." He paused. "And the book?"

"I pulled the plug." He let out an anguished groan.

"It's not like you have a cut from the profits. Why do you care?"

"You can't just throw it away! Can you?"

"Yes, I can! I don't want to use people any more. I built this whole damn book around Shane. I can't. . ." I trailed off.

"What!" He snapped.

"I came to my senses." I could hear him shake his head over the phone. He was now speechless. "I can't do it. I don't want to be that person." I hung up the phone, and I don't think I'm ever going to speak to him again.

(Later)

I'm glad that the subscribers don't have my personal e-mail, because I just perused the message boards, and they are livid. One thread contained an endless stream of "What the fuck?" and "Death to Jed Haele" titled rants. "I hope that he contracts an illness that involves bleeding from every orifice," one person wrote. Another one speculated that my career was a scam. "Jed stole two unpublished novels in order to build up a following, and then collected the windfall of anticipation of a third novel. He tried to do it, and when he realized that he was incapable, he dumped us. It's a fucking scam," he wrote. At least ten included some variation of "He can go to Haele" in their diatribes.

Obviously, none of my fans read the newspaper. I didn't mention it in the message to the subscribers, because I assumed that they were aware of current events. What do they do with their lives? Don't they read newspapers or watch the news? Is my fiction THE focus of their existence?

August 11, 2003

While I was in the shower this morning, the detective called me. I almost slipped on the tiles as I bolted across the kitchen floor to answer the phone. "Mr. Heely?"

"It's Haele, sir. It rhymes with the ice that falls from the sky during a summer storm."

"Ahem." He coughed. "You haven't heard from Mr. Lasch, have you?"

"No."

He coughed again and hacked up something, with his mouth as close to the receiver as possible. "Sorry," he rasped. "If you do, please give me a call at—"

I cut him off. "I have your number somewhere."

"Uh-huh. Well, why don't you let me remind you, son," he drawled, suddenly. "This is a serious sit-chi-ay-shun." Where did they get this detective from? Was there some sort of detective exchange program I am not aware of involving New York City and rural West Virginia?

"Yes, sir."

"Once again my number is 555-6660. Now don't forget to dial the '212.' That's compulsory now."

"Compulsory."

He cackled, a bit mockingly. "Just dropping my word of the day on you, son. Now, don't you forget that number. Did you write it down?"

"Of course." I lied.

August 18, 2003

Now that my novel (or rather, novella? Long short story?) has a much more abrupt ending, I decided to take the sort of chances that I could not have considered before. Instead of releasing the brief chapter as written, I am adding on a grisly conclusion. After Sean slaps the alien and it bleeds white blood, Sean will feel an uncontrollable desire to suck on the white blood that drips down Julian's flattening cheek. While Julian's race of aliens have strong psychic powers, they are quite frail physically. His cheek bleeds the toothpaste-like blood faster and faster, and the flesh turns gray. Sean cups the creamy blood in his hands and drinks it.

He can't help himself and proceeds to consume the dying alien's body. It ends with him dragging the rotting, dead remains up to his apartment.

August 19, 2003

Shelby was the apex. I never topped myself. Just like Bram Stoker's ***Dracula***, the titular character stayed in the shadows and had precious few appearances in the text. I just barely pulled the subtlety thing off.

Dance of the Damned was a failure in successful clothing. The Versace fit well and I applied a nice perfume to it, but it was shit without true intricacy. It was a puzzle with pieces that did not fit together at the end. My attempt at an ironic conclusion was too silly.

August 20, 2003

I stayed home last night and drank vodka with a bag of generic brand cashews that had a vague banana flavor.

I called Janine this afternoon and told her that the chapter was ready. "Finally! You do know that I start school in two weeks."

"Oh." Did she know? "Have you, um?" I trailed off and then cracked my jaw.

"You're nervous." She paused. "I go to your website occasionally."

"So you?"

"Yep!"

"So?"

She exhaled into the receiver. "It's been good, and it will be good. The ending of it all. That final chapter?"

"Oh, hunny! Don't be so cryptic." I tried to break the tension.

"It's fine."

"Of course you shouldn't assume that it's over," I added to soften the blow.

"But it is."

"Yeah, it is over. I can't write fiction anymore. I can do the journal, but not fiction."

"How does it end?"

"You'll see. It's not too long, so you should be able to do it in a few days, at most. I want to distribute it over the holiday weekend. It'll give those workers something to look forward to."

August 22, 2003

Let's be frank today.

I gave up two careers this week. One was a vestige of my past. The origins of the other career were more contemporary, and it was entirely of my creation. They both ended voluntarily and abruptly, and I couldn't be happier.

I can't work for Dad anymore, because I don't want to live a life where all my success was rooted in nepotism. That path leads to resentment from coworkers and a lifelong paranoia that I am unable to stand on my own two feet. It is hell. That cannot be my life.

August 23, 2003

Now I am having fucked up dreams.

Beatrice called me late in the day at work at Sterling Subs, and I was very busy. "I want to read the ending now!" she said. It was late afternoon, and I was livid. We had run out of Sterling Silver Sauce and Nuclear Cheddar cheese bread. I glared at my assistant while I held the phone to me ear. "I need to read it!" she demanded.

"Okay. Okay! I'll get Chester to cover for me. I'll meet you at my place in an hour."

I got to my apartment first. I skimmed my chapter while I waited. I hated every word. She opened the door with her key.

"You don't have a key," I said. In real life, she doesn't have one.

She ignored my remark and collapsed on my couch. She was at least twenty pounds lighter. Her skin was clear.

"What drugs are you on?" I asked.

"I can't handle this. I'm a fucking monster now."

"I am too," I said.

She shook her head. "You're sweeter than anybody. I can always count on that dick and your ass. They're lovely. Can you stand up and turn around for me. Let me see it in those jeans."

"You sound like a gay man, Beatrice."

She stood up and pulled off her face, revealing Dean's face underneath. "I am a gay man!"

I woke up in my bed screaming. I have spent way too much time by myself in my apartment the last few weeks. I allowed the stench of death to ravage me. It's the odor from the chemicals they used to clean up the mess Dean's corpse made by my door. It smells like melting plastic and rancid meat.

August 24, 2003

Today was an improvement.

I paced down Ninth Avenue. That avenue is as sprawling as the city gets. It was very sunny, but cool as well. The familiar or possibly conditioned feeling of vague nausea or anxiety that I still associate with late summer (due to the countdown to the fall semester of school in years past) haunted my walk, but I knew that I was now long free of that cycle. That made me feel a little better. I went to the Cheyenne Diner on Ninth Avenue.

Two girls immediately intrigued me. The one facing me as I entered was black, with a kind face and gray eyes. She performed a subtle and unfamiliar dance move with her upper body while seated at the booth, and the girl opposite her let out a throaty laugh. "Don't laugh, Juliana! You saw it last night. They haven't a clue. Those . . ." She paused and glanced at me as I passed by. "Yankees?"

I grinned and sat myself in the next booth with my back to them and eavesdropped.

"Cheyenne! You have to give them some slack."

She scoffed. "It pisses me off. If they shook their asses like that in Lock, they would be laughed all the way out of the county."

Juliana laughed. "Cheyenne!" she yelled.

Cheyenne shook her hair, and it brushed over my neck. She turned around and sweetly apologized.

"Aw, don't mention it," I said.

"Why don't you join us?" Cheyenne asked.

"Cheyenne?" I remarked and then stood up. "You do know that's the name of?"

She interrupted and giggled. "Of course, sweetie."

I sat beside her. Juliana was few years older than Cheyenne. "You'll have to excuse my friend. This is her first time away from home, since, um . . ." Juliana trailed off.

I turned to Cheyenne, and she just shrugged her shoulders. "It's no big deal, Jules. I'm adopted. I may have been born elsewhere, but I still consider myself a native of Lock, Virginia."

"Virginia?" They nodded. "Now I know someone, or rather two people from Virginia." They nodded some more and smiled.

The friendly waitress, elfin and smirking, brought out their food now. I took over the conversation while they ate.

"When do you ladies go home?" I asked.

"We're pretty laid back about that," Juliana said. "Cheyenne's never been away from home, and my dad wants Cheyenne to have a good time, so he really helped us out with money. We just got here, so?"

"I'm laid back too." I sat up real straight.

"Do you know your way around the city?" Juliana asked.

This saddened me a bit. "I do," I said curtly.

"Well, then?"

"Does she have an ID?" I asked, and they nodded.

"I may have never left Lock before, but I have seen the inside of a few bars!" Cheyenne said.

I directed the conversation toward Lock to divert from Juliana's question, and they obliged. It's a town with a population of 197 people. There is one Main Street, and it's called Lock Avenue. Apparently there is more money in the town than one would expect. Juliana leaked this with pride. "My father, Jake Banyon, owns a steakhouse that is so popular that he is barraged daily by investors who want him to open even more locations."

"Jake Banyon is your dad?"

She blushed. "Yeah."

"That's part of the reason why we're here. He wants us to go to both of the New York City locations." She paused and gulped the remainder of her Coke. "It's for fun, um . . . ."

"Jed Haele," I said.

"You're not Jed Haele?"

"Oh, yeah. I'm him." This almost never happens.

Cheyenne looked at us, confused. "How do you know his last name like that?"

"He used to be a writer," she said to Cheyenne. "My mom was so pissed off at you!" she said to me and then turned back to Cheyenne. "He didn't finish his last book. You see . . ." Juliana described my process. She explained how the online subscribership worked and concluded with a play-by-play about the aborted third novel.

"Virginia? I didn't know that I had readers so far away from New York. Wow!"

"My mom read ***Shelby*** and was instantly hooked."

"Everybody liked that one," I added.

"Why did you stop?"

"It was too much work and I was running out of ideas." I decided not to be forthcoming about my final novel or the murder.

"That makes sense."

"Exactly," I said. "By the way, the last chapter will be out next weekend. Your mom will love it. I promise."

"First thing's first," Juliana interrupted. "Do you know your way around the city?" she asked again.

"Not lately," I said grimly. "I've been too busy with the last chapter."

"Well, I don't want to spend two weeks at Daddy's restaurants. I want to have fun!"

Cheyenne grinned. "We do. We really do."

"Okay. The clubs are best on weeknights, so our timing is good. Tomorrow is Monday. We can go to Frozen Poison. I like to eat before I go to the clubs. The Capitol Diner is good, and it's only ten blocks away from the club."

"What about right now?" Cheyenne asked.

I laughed. "You're really chomping at the bit. If you girls really have nothing better to do, then I could give you a walking tour. This is my favorite part of the city. Thirty-fifth through Fiftieth Street are so dense with memories for me. It's a shame you didn't come in the fall. There is nothing more beautiful than Bryant Park in the fall on an overcast afternoon."

We went to Bryant Park, and it was too crowded, but we found a table in the shade. "They'll have the fashion shows here in two weeks," I said.

"We'll miss them," Juliana said.

"I want to miss them," I said. "I'm so over it."

"Lock is a nice place to live. It's so pretty," Juliana said.

"THIS is pretty!" Cheyenne said. "I want to go to school here." Juliana and I laughed. "What?"

We laughed at her for different reasons. Juliana explained that Cheyenne's mother would "not let her live," if she opted to go to school in New York City. She would "harass her with endless long-distance calls." I nodded along with her rationale, but I laughed for another reason. Cheyenne wants to be an urban girl. She has the stars in her eyes and craves my lifestyle. She'd have to stop eating, start fucking, stop smiling from joy, start smiling from contempt, and get rich immediately.

This process destroys people. I've seen it firsthand. The roads leading to THE major cities are littered with girls and boys who fall short. Some of them have scars that will last a lifetime. Simon is a good male example of this. They disintegrate, piece by piece. They destroy themselves.

I laughed along with Juliana even though my reason was clearly different from hers. I laughed because Cheyenne has no idea what the lifestyle she craves entails. I laughed at the absurdity of her wish. Thankfully neither of them thought it through and asked for my reason.

Juliana, Cheyenne, and I went to her dad's restaurant, which was about seven blocks above Times Square in the Fifties. It's a dark steak restaurant, which would have been very smoky before the ban. It still smelled a bit like a bowling alley. Since it was crowded, we opted to eat at the bar. Juliana sat between Cheyenne and I.

"What do you recommend, Juliana?"

"Any steak. If you want fish, then the lobster tails should be good."

I perused the menu. "How about the 'Curried Pork Chop'? That's a bit incongruent with the rest of the menu, and the theme of the place."

"Yeah, it is," Juliana said.

"Take it as a hint," Cheyenne added.

"That's so weird."

Juliana flipped to the dessert menu at the back. "I love the apple crisp," she said.

"I'll get the brownie thing."

She laughed. "How do you know they have a brownie thing?"

"They always have a brownie thing," I said.

I also ordered the lobster tails and they were quite good. I'm amazed that I've overlooked the place for so long. They said that there's another one in Chelsea. "It's not as successful as this location." The girls discussed the food quality quite a bit. "The pasta is too soft and the shrimp were dried out," Juliana said about her dish, and she reiterated it with every other bite. "The bigger problem is the side dishes, Juliana. They overdid it on the butter in these mashed potatoes." Cheyenne flattened them out with her fork. "They are too shiny."

Juliana pushed her food away. "This stinks. Dad's suspicions about the food here are true. He will be so disappointed."

"I know about that. I frequently disappoint my dad."

"He won't be disappointed in me. He will be disappointed by the news," Juliana said. "Why did you interpret it that way?"

"That's why I think I need to get away. I see too much negativity."

"You are so over it," Cheyenne suggested.

Her echo of my statement from earlier startled me a bit. "Maybe I need to go to Cali or Lock, Virginia," I said. Cheyenne smiled. "That would be so awesome. I could run away and start fresh." I paused. "And I already know two people who live there."

From the Journal of Juliana Banyon

August 26, 2003

We arrived early at the nearly empty Capitol Diner for the Monday night jaunt. The owner stood behind the cash register. Behind him was a large mirror with a bar in front of it. Dozens of bottles of liquor cluttered this counter. He smiled and led us to a small booth. "I would prefer that table. We are expecting at least one more person." I pointed to the large table in the back of the dining room.

"This table is not good," he said with a slight accent. "Oh, wait a minute. You're with Jed. You're here early. They usually show up around nine. You can wait there if you like." He walked us over. As we sat down on the heavily worn wooden chairs, something peculiar occurred to me: why would he know Jed by name?

I asked him, and his response surprised me. "Jed worked for me when he was in college." This struck me as absurd for two reasons: First, Jed was a rich kid. He didn't need to work. Secondly, if he chose to work, one would think he would have picked something more glamorous. As I pondered this, he walked away.

Soon after, Jed arrived with Janine. I avoided the topic in front of his friend because I felt he might be embarrassed by his old job.

They ordered appetizers and ate fast. Cheyenne and I split a chicken gyro platter while they conversed. I tuned them out. Suddenly, Janine raised her voice. "You aren't playing fair with them, Jed!"

He grabbed her hand and nodded grimly. "We need to let this drop, Janine. We really do."

She exhaled hard and shook her head. Then, she looked me in the eye. "Not you guys," she said softly. "It's not about you. Jed and I have disagreements, but . . ."

Jed laughed. "Let's just say that Janine and I are drinking to forget tonight!"

"Exactly."

Shortly after that, the four of us emerged from the diner. We walked about five blocks and stopped at a small and quiet bar. An aging red-haired waitress served us drinks. While I sipped my bourbon, Jed and Janine conversed with the waitress. Her name was Gloria. They clearly had known each other for some time. She stood behind Jed and put her hands on his shoulders. "Now, I've seen many handsome boys in my life, but Jed is the cutest of the bunch."

Jed smiled. "Sure, babe. I feel the love," he said, still smiling.

"Gloria likes 'em young," the bartender cackled from behind the bar.

"Fuck off," she snarled back at him.

"We like you, Gloria," Janine said. "You are pretty hot for thirty-seven."

"Thanks. You guys make me feel twenty-one again." Jed turned his head around to face her alone. He may have mouthed some words or given her a facial gesture. Either way, she walked away smiling. It was almost ten and he probably felt it was time to leave.

As we strutted out of the bar, she emerged again just in time to watch us walk away. We walked at least ten more blocks, and Cheyenne complained that her feet hurt. "This is New York, babe. All we do is walk," Jed said. "The diner is twenty blocks from the club. I think I said ten yesterday, but—"

"Capitol Diner to Frozen Poison?" Janine said. "That's a twenty–two-block walk, Jed."

"Sorry, girls," he said to Cheyenne and I. He leaned into me and whispered, "No more inhibitions. That's what it's all about." We turned down a dark side street. It was deserted, yet I heard muffled music coming from the grimy industrial buildings surrounding us. Suddenly, I saw a small light blue door lamp. Jed stopped and everybody crowded around the light.

I was confused. "Why is nobody out here?"

"The line is inside, and it will be crowded." He opened the door and held it for us. Inside there was an elevator. It arrived just moments later, and the elevator operator greeted us. To my surprise, it descended. I realized that the music was coming from below ground all along. The door opened and we exited to a waiting area. There was a huge line. Jed led us past the line and headed for the doorman.

Jed had a brief dialogue with the doorman, and we bypassed the line and went inside. The doorman wore black sunglasses and black leather. He pulled up his shades and flashed a slight smirk at me as I walked in.

Frozen Poison was insane. In the three levels, one could find almost any imaginable scene. There was a bar on each level. On the lower entry level, there was a huge dance floor. Scores of beautiful people moved with the intoxicating techno beat. I separated from my friends. They said something about getting a table upstairs and went up a spiral staircase. I wanted to explore. As I advanced, a dark-haired beauty who looked like a porcelain doll grabbed me. "What's your name?" I yelled. "Makiko," she said. Both her and the music pulled me deeper into the multitude of people. We stopped somewhere in the middle, and she pushed herself into me. As I reciprocated, the music grew increasingly frenzied as the climax of the song approached. Everything moved faster and faster. "I'm not a lesbian!" I yelled. Another woman pushed into me from behind. Some of her orange hair flung into my face. I turned around, and she was grinning with delight. As I pulled toward her, Makiko disappeared. I thrust my chest over hers as she groped the flesh of my back violently. The music stopped abruptly and started up again before anyone could notice the gap. I scanned her body through her tight green dress. "Priscilla," I moaned and rested my head in her chest. The name was printed over her chest. She released me from her tight grasp, and I looked up at her. "I'm Juliana," I said.

"That's not my name," she said and giggled. I stood up straight and pulled her arm as we left the dance floor.

"Ecstasy?" she asked.

The drug or the feeling? It was the drug, but I momentarily thought it was the feeling, and I almost embarrassed myself, but stopped before I made a dumb comment.

I followed her upstairs. The second level had a larger bar and tables. All the walls were painted in solid primary colors. I walked with her to a dark red corner, where there was a door. She pushed through it. Just as the door closed behind her, I walked in. It was a bathroom. She advanced and talked to a male drug dealer in the corner to the left of the door. "Pris," I yelled.

"Who the hell are you calling a pris, motherfucker?" the grim-looking dealer said. "My name is Cecil, bitch!" The long gray coat he wore made him look even more menacing. He abruptly put his hand inside his deep pocket.

As he lunged toward me and pulled something out from the pocket, Priscilla grabbed him. "Wait, man!" Priscilla yelled. "Look." She pointed to her chest. He turned around and looked at her. He found the faux pas hysterical and let out a demented chuckle, and they continued their business. Based on the expression I saw on her face as I walked out of the room, he gave her a good deal. I was still shaking from the narrowly evaded attack. I leaned against the red wall outside of the bathroom and slowly regained my composure while I waited for her to emerge.

The door flew open again, and she grabbed my arm. "Drinks," she said and pointed at the bar. "I'll get us a good table." I got two beers and went to the table she picked out. The table overlooked the dance floor below. When I sat down, she put a pill in my hand. I rolled it around in my palm and she smiled at me. "You want to know my real name?" I nodded. "It's Beatrice."

"Bea."

She rolled her eyes. "Ick. Don't call me that. Beatrice is already a repulsive name. The short version is even more disgusting."

"Sorry. By the way, I am not a lesbian."

"You're bisexual?"

"Approximately," I said cryptically. It was an odd word choice.

She laughed. "That's a new one, babe."

"Don't call me babe."

She laughed. "You like Shampoo?"

"Huh?"

"The band."

"I never heard of them." I popped the pill and washed it down with my beer. "You know, Priscilla, I was determined to stay relatively sober tonight, so I could see and hear everything I encounter."

She nodded and grinned. "You're about to fail at that." I watched her take the drug. Her neck muscles pulsed as the liquid went down her throat. "Let's chill here until it kicks in." I nodded.

Maybe an hour later, I felt very peppy. Words seemed like a waste of time. I never felt more distracted in my life. Time seemed too restrictive, and I wished everything would just move faster. Then, it seemed like things were speeding up. "As in Presley?" I asked at some point.

"Nah, I just like the name. Nothing against Elvis though. He is hot."

"Isn't he, like, dead?" I asked jokingly, and we both laughed.

"Wanna go up," she asked. She pointed her thin hand toward the spiral staircase.

"What's there?"

"Let's see. I don't know myself." As we walked up the spiraling stairs, I held onto the cold metal banister. I swayed a little from dizziness. The effects of the E were overwhelming me somewhat. The pill had much less of an effect on her. She ascended faster than I did, and by the time she reached the top, I was barely halfway there. "Aw, how unoriginal. It's another orgy. That's practically what they had downstairs," she said grimly. I sped up.

When I reached the top of the stairs, I saw Jed nearby. His eyes lingered over the bodies of the three women who crowded around him. One of them offered him a cigarette as he removed her bra. "No thanks, baby. I can't smoke anything. I'm a track star," he moaned as she groped him. The music was much softer on this floor. Beatrice led me through this and stopped when we reached her friend. Makiko was thrusting herself against another woman from behind. They were kneeling down on the floor. The shoulder straps of her dress had fallen down, and she wasn't wearing a bra.

Makiko's new girlfriend smiled at me, and I walked forward. She grabbed me gently with her arms and pulled me closer. I looked up and away. Then I felt her soft face rubbing into my rough black jeans. "No more inhibitions. That's what it's all about." Jed's words echoed in my mind, and I looked down and put my hands on her shoulders. I moved back, tore my blouse and bra off, and threw them up in the air. I didn't care where they landed. Nobody else had done that! Makiko picked up my clothes. She put my gray shirt over her dress. Then, Beatrice, Makiko, the new girl, and I went to the private rooms.

A few hours later, I sat on the middle level at a table with Jed and Janine. Makiko and Beatrice were at a nearby table drinking margaritas. We sat in a row, and all three of us could see Makiko and Beatrice. The girls decided to arrange it so that they could see and hear me talk about them with my guy friend. While Jed described his exploits, I occasionally glanced at Makiko and Beatrice.

"You wouldn't believe what I did, Jed," I said, when it seemed like Jed had run out of stories to tell.

Jed turned all his attention to me. "I saw some of it and wonder how far you went," he said with keenness in his eyes. Makiko smiled. She focused her dark eyes on Jed as she listened. Jed did not notice that she was staring at him. "You met some strangers and did a bang-up job."

"You took the words right out of my mouth, Jed."

"I doubt you would have been so crass," he suggested.

"Is that a challenge?" I asked huskily. "I met two beautiful girls on the dance floor. Eventually we reached the third floor and had a quadruple banger in a private room on 3."

Jed interrupted. "Makiko," he said. He looked at her slyly. "I told you she would be easy. Though what is the deal with this kinky game?"

"Just trying something new, Jed," she purred in a fake French accent.

"I'm not a lesbian," I added. "I'm bisexual."

Jed laughed. "I knew that. Cheyenne told me. She wanted to give me a fair warning."

"Fuck me!" I hit myself on the forehead. "What happened to Cheyenne?"

Jed and Janine laughed. "She left very early. She's too young for this," Jed said.

Makiko and Beatrice joined us at our table. "Hey, kids," Makiko said.

"How goes it, ladies?"

"Very nice," Beatrice said. "Though did you hear about Cecil?"

"No," Jed said.

Beatrice shook her head. "He got into an awful fight with someone and they had to take them to the hospital."

"You know Cecil?" I asked.

Jed laughed. "Sure. Everyone knows Cecil." He paused. "He always gets into fights, ladies. It goes with his job."

"This one was much worse. The guy shattered Cecil's shoulder to bits and broke enough ribs to cause internal bleeding. That's the story going around."

"Yikes!"

Makiko sighed. "Bea and I are heading off. We like your new friend, Jed. She's a real dish."

"Where are you headed?" I asked.

"We're going to Pussy Go Lure," Beatrice said.

"Seriously?" Jed asked. "Is that a new place?" He flashed them a confused look. "Is that a real place?"

They laughed and walked away.

Jed, Janine, and I left around 2:45. "Where are we going next?" I asked.

"You want more?" Jed asked. "Our next stop will have more of a drug crowd. In addition, they've got louder and faster music. It's called Eclectic."

"The name is dead-on accurate. It's really trippy. It is almost like entering a dream world," Janine said.

We walked through town in silence for a few minutes. Jed chose a path and led us through many side streets. Some were empty. Others were crowded with people trying to get into various clubs.

To be perfectly honest, I was somewhat bored. The drugs amplified this feeling, as I was starting the descent from the drugs I took earlier. Everything was slowing down. When we stopped at the door of Eclectic, I thought to myself "So what?" My comrades, picked up on this, took immediate measures to rectify the situation once we were inside. "She needs a pick-me-up," Janine said to Jed. "Look at her." Jed stared at me for a moment and frowned. "We'll score her some uppers inside. She's fine," he said. I was conscious. However, I felt indifferent and detached.

When we walked through the doors of Eclectic, the environment was an intense sensory barrage. Jed paced ahead of us and left me with Janine. I stopped a few feet past the door and stood in deep crimson light with her. Moments later, Jed stepped out of greenness and turned red as he approached us. "C'mon, I have something for you," he said. As I walked with them, the music slowed down. He led us to a VIP table on the second level. When we got there, I looked down and saw the place much more clearly. The dance floor below us was packed. There were costumed performers on at least a half-dozen elevated platforms. Janine grinned at us and bolted for the dance floor. "I'll be back with a man!" she yelled.

Jed and I sat at the table alone. He pulled out an orange pill and handed it to me. "Are you in over your head?" he asked.

"Nah," I said with bombast while grabbing the pill from him.

"I never met somebody who was so willing to take drugs without asking questions."

"You never met someone like me who was so uninhibited?"

Jed sighed. "Yeah, that's what I meant. It's cool if you can handle it."

"I bet you can always count on a wild time when Jed is around," I said.

I looked at the orange pill in my hand and said, "I don't think I am going to need this. I don't feel weird anymore."

"Keep it. Just in case you need some energy later."

I held the pill up to the light. "Energy? What would I need that for?" I said and then laughed. "Besides, I like drinking better."

"You'll learn," he said.

A very bizarre woman approached the table, and her appearance initially made me think my high was really kicking in. She had a very sloppy dark blonde wig on, a cheesy 80s-era blouse and skintight blue leather pants. She had a ton of poorly applied makeup on her face and dark sunglasses with big lenses. I assumed she was a trashy drag queen. She abruptly sat next to Jed and moved in real close to him. "Hey, baby," she said and stared him straight in the eye. Jed was too stunned, so he just nodded. "I'm Sharlee Jean."

I looked at her, confused. "Charly Sheen?" I asked.

She shook her head and the wig did not even move close to in sync with her head. "Sharlee Jean! Sharlee Jean!" she barked at me and waved her hand. She resumed staring at Jed. "What you doin', baby?" she asked.

"Um . . .," he stammered.

"Calm down, I got what you want. I dressed just so you could see I got what you want." She pushed her drink in front of him. "You can try my Ho."

"Your what?"

"My drank!" she yelled. "Hennessy and orange soda. It's my drank, baby."

"Oh."

"You ain't got a lot to say, huh? Well . . ." She trailed off and grabbed his hand. She brought it down to feel her ass, and he pulled it right back. "Oh, I am all cleaned out for you, baby. I ate prunes and brown rice all day yesterday. I am all pooped out and open and ready for your nice fat cock."

Jed was stunned and incapable of responding or rejecting her. Frankly, I was a little surprised. I leaned into Jed's other side and licked his neck. He turned to face me and smiled and mouthed, "Thank you."

Sharlee pursed her lips and shook her head in a huff. "Enjoy that pale constipated bitch, dickwad!" She stood up and skulked off.

"What, EXACTLY, was that?" I asked.

"I think she is a hooker on crystal meth," Jed said.

"Funny. I thought she was a very trashy drag queen."

"Maybe both?"

A few minutes later, Janine appeared with a bright and bubbly boy who was heavily drugged. His outward appearance did not suggest this. However, when he began to talk it was obvious he was strung out. "I am like way totally stoned, Justice. What was that? You rock! Who are they?" he said each sentence as though it were a separate entity of its own.

Jed looked at him and smiled. "It's Janine, dear. Your new lady friend's name is Janine." He nodded slowly. "Do you want to play some more, Janine?" Jed asked Janine. She shook her head. "I want to leave too. I feel strange tonight. Let's get a cab and go to my parents' house," he said.

"They're away this week?" Janine asked.

"Yeah."

"Where is it?" I asked.

"All the way out on Long Island," Jed said.

Janine's new boy toy did not stir at all the entire drive back. Our conversation proved so engaging that the sudden sight of Jed's imposing house frightened me. Its pale blue–colored bricks glowed eerily against the blackness of the night.

We walked through the house in darkness and Jed went to the large living room in the back of the first floor, which overlooked the pool. He dropped his keys on a table and turned on the lights. The room was immense.

"Is your fucking brother here?" Janine asked.

"Nope," Jed said.

"Thank fucking God!"

Jed and I settled on the huge white couch by the window. He pretended to look at the pool outside. Then he turned to face me and touched my brown hair. This was all about having fun. As both of us stripped, we felt guiltless splendor. The entire night was about guiltless splendor.

From the Journal of Jed Haele

August 25, 2003

Janine was in a shitty mood today. She came to my apartment earlier than expected. About a half hour after my very late lunch, she rang the doorbell. I stared at her through the peephole too long, and she did not look amused.

"Open up!" she yelled.

I opened the door. She was dressed for our outing. She wore a fitted olive-colored dress. "You're early," I said.

"Yeah," she said. She went to my dining table and took a seat. "I think you need to rewrite it." She pulled the chapter out of her handbag. "They. Will. Hate. It." She paused between each word.

"It's too late."

She shook her head. "No, it's not. You can stay home tonight and fix the fucking thing."

"Janine, just do your job."

"I am not the writer."

"You are not listening to me, Janine. This is over. You can do whatever you want to it. I don't care anymore. You know that."

"Okay, Jed, but we need to go through it. I need guidance from you in order to effectively do my job."

"Fine."

We went through the chapter line by line and openly mocked it. This took seven hours. "You know that I don't care anymore," I reiterated when we were done. She nodded. "Okay." I took a deep breath. "Polish it! Cut it! Rearrange it! Whatever!"

"I will do my best," she said grimly.

"Good. I need to get fucked up now!"

August 26, 2003

The clubbing sucked. I arranged to go with Janine, Juliana, and Cheyenne. Makiko and Beatrice arrived separately before we got to Frozen Poison. Makiko and Bea pounced on Juliana.

Cheyenne was petrified by the dance floor and hid near the door. I bought her a beer and tried to calm her down, but she was trembling. "I don't like this," she said. I held my arm around her shoulder, walked her outside, and hailed a cab.

When I went back inside, Juliana was STILL all over the girls. She blew me off for at least two hours. She couldn't get enough of the girls.

That's why it's so surprising that she had sex with me. We went to my parents' house and I fucked her on the couch.

Chester woke me up this morning. "Damn! That bitch was hot."

"Where is she?" I asked.

"She just left. Did you shag that ass good?" he asked and then chortled. I slowly sat up and glared at him. "You hung over? Damn!"

"Yeah." I scoffed. "I'm hung . . ." I trailed off. He laughed again. "Oh, fuck off," I said. My head was pounding.

He rhythmically shifted his shoulders back and forth, and I realized that reggae music was playing in a nearby room, possibly the dining room? "Dad's here," he said.

"Oh, fuck me!" I said. He didn't make a crack about that one because I know how to say that one and he doesn't. It's a tough curse to pull off, but it sounds cool if you can do it. Otherwise, it's weird. "Is Janine and . . . some guy still here?"

"No Janine, but the dude is still here. He's in your room. He was walking around the hall upstairs like a zombie before."

"Ugh. Do me a favor. Get him into my room and tell him it's time to go sleepy sleep some more. Make sure he lies down, and then lock him in. I think I have to deal with Dad first."

"He's at the pool."

I turned around and saw him out there. He sat at the table by the pool and was drinking coffee. He was so tan.

"Take care of it, and I'll buy you a case of beer."

"Okey dokes," he said and left.

"Yep," I said softly. Then, I stood up. I was still wearing a black silk shirt and the tight gray jeans that sculpted my crotch and toned ass. I looked down, and thankfully, there was no dry semen on me! I grabbed a pair of sunglasses that were lying on the coffee table and went outside.

I smiled and headed for the table. "You're back!"

He frowned. "We intended to return after Labor Day. Then I got your message."

I sat down. "Yeah," I said.

He pushed the coffee across the table and leaned forward. "It's not acceptable. I heard about your friend Gene, but that's not an excuse to turn your back on my business." He paused and exhaled hard. "No, that is not acceptable at all."

"You can't understand, Dad. You don't have friends."

He shook his head. "Welcome to the club, kiddo. That's the way that it goes."

"Way it goes," I whispered bitterly. "Way it goes."

"Don't get me wrong. Gene was nice enough, but I'm sure that you would have parted ways eventually."

"His name was Dean."

"Okay. That's not the point. You need to be serious about your career. You need to get your shit together now. You need to go back to work, or else you will have to fend for yourself. You will not enjoy that. You are five years away from thirty. It does not get better. It gets worse every year, even if you are a success. The ONLY way to ameliorate that is to be serious. You do not want to wake up at thirty and realize that you fucked up. I have offered you serious opportunities, Jed."

"Running a fucking sandwich shop? Chester could do that."

"Yeah, and he will. Then I'll invite him to my offices." He paused. "That's how it works. You don't want to put in the time. Maybe he is more patient and serious than you. Maybe you both are fuck ups?" He paused again. "What I am telling you right now is that this is an exploding offer."

I was rapidly losing this argument. "How much longer do I have to work in the shop?"

He nodded and grinned. "I think that I told you it would take three years when you finished school. Next June will be three years. I will knock five months off. You can come to work in my offices in January. The salary will be 125. That's 35 more than I gave my last hire six years ago, and he was an MBA." He chuckled. "He's up to 135 now, so I will save ten when I fire him and replace him with you."

I tried to compose myself, but my lip twitched. "When do you need to know?"

"I'll give you a week."

From the Journal of Fiona Haele

August 29, 2003

I had a nightmare and woke up just past 3:00 a.m. We got home from dinner late last night. My hair was all crinkled and frizzy and sweaty and all over my face as I abruptly woke up. I pulled it back, away from my face, as I sat up in bed. It took me a minute to catch my breath. I grabbed Seymour's arm, and he eased awake, as he does.

"Yes," he said with his husky and gravelly voice. He grabbed the remnants of the joint he started before bed and lit up.

"It's Jed."

"What about him?"

"I just had the worst nightmare about him."

"That's nothing new. You have bad dreams about the kids all the time."

"This one was worse." He nodded and sighed. "Seymour! Could you at least pretend like you could care fucking less?" He put the joint in the ashtray and mimed popping a pill. "It's not that, and I have to take that medication." He nodded, smugly.

I tried to describe the dream to him, but he cut me off and suggested I call Jed tomorrow and tell him all about it.

I won't do that, and I can't sleep now, so I am going to write about it here.

Jesse, Chester, Janine, Dean, two other women, and I were at his apartment. Jed and Dean suddenly held Janine down on his couch and Chester went to the kitchen and got a blowtorch. He came back and held it to her nose and she writhed and screamed as he held it there with no emotion on his face at all as if he was in a trance. Then they let her go, and Jed and Dean laughed the sickest laughs you have ever heard in your life. Their cackles were inhuman. She ran away to the kitchen.

I sat stunned on the chair, and the two girls started pacing in that same kind of trance about the room. Then, Janine came back with two towels. She held one to her nose. She paused at the threshold as the two girls passed in the midst of their pacing and then she lunged for Chester. The towel dropped from her hand and she raised it with a long knife and sliced open Chester's throat! She cut him open, and the blood splashed all over them.

Jed nodded in approval and rubbed the blood into his face and his white shirt. He smirked and raised his arms at his sides, and everyone paused, except Chester, who fell to the floor dying. I was suddenly paralyzed. He dropped his arms, and kneeled down and grasped at Chester's throat to pool more blood in his hands, and then the ran it through his hair to slick it back. His entire face was also caked in blood, and his stark, shiny, white pupils glowed ever so slightly.

He placed his bloody hand on his pants, and his hand trembled slightly, but it became more of a vibration, and it went up his arm. The girls resumed pacing, and Dean went to Jed's desk by the window.

Jed stood up. His entire arm was vibrating now. He started to speak in tongues. It moved so violently that it seemed that the bones in his shoulder could break, and then he violently turned his body around to face his desk, and I saw Dean emerge from it with a black gun. Jed spoke gibberish faster and raised his vibrating arm in the direction of the two girls, who were on the far side of the room by the window. Dean fired a single bullet at one of their heads, and a brief splash of blood in the air preceded her abrupt fall to the ground. Dean ran over to her and rubbed her blood over his face and hair just like Jed did as the second girl stood there in a trance. Jed nodded and continued mumbling.

They gathered behind Jed. Jed's unintelligible mumbling suddenly turned into words. "We have so much more to do," he said and then paused. He licked some blood off his finger. "NOW!" Then, Jed turned his gaze to me, as they paced toward me.

Suddenly, I could see Janine was fighting through his mind control and pain from her swelling and burnt face. She slowly raised her arm with the knife. Jed winked at me and then had a vastly stronger control over her. Her face went blank, and she raced up to me and stabbed me in the chest. I didn't feel a thing, and then the blood spewed out all over the four of them.

I was dying and they slowly left the apartment. On their way out, I heard screaming on the other side of the wall. It sounded like a man beating a woman to death . . . and then I heard something similar coming from the apartment above us . . . and then below us. The screams grew louder and louder until I woke up.

From the Journal of Barry Bowman

August 26, 2003

On my way to Seymour Haele's office, I passed the many nameless people whose jobs here were far below mine. At the end of the corridor was an empty desk. The secretary had left for the day. I bit the bullet and pushed open the door to face the inevitable.

A woman sat next to Seymour, and this added discomfort to the situation. Her hair was combed with military precision. ***My replacement?*** I thought.

Seymour spun around in his chair, revealing his wizened face. His grave expression coupled with the presence of this similarly severe-looking stranger immediately informed me of the dead serious tone of what would follow.

"Why don't you just get to the point? What's the upshot, sir?" I asked. Sensing that Seymour was about to fire me, I no longer felt the need to be polite.

He spoke in a dry monotone. "You are an asset, Barry. I am sure that your true value can be actualized in . . ."

I smirked at him, and he paused. I no longer allowed the hideous dynamic of employer and employee to restrain my contempt. "Who the fuck is she, Seymour?" I asked.

This blatant abandonment of respect made Seymour uncomfortable. His normally domineering tone and diction disintegrated into a fleeting effort to get out his pre-planned words. "I am sure that you . . . your value . . . your true value will be actualized . . . It can be actualized in another job."

"Who the fuck is she, Seymour?" I asked again. She stopped gazing into space at this point and stared straight at me. "Perfect! Just perfect! She is here as a voyeur to the slaughter. Don't look at me like that. You don't have the decency, or the guts for that matter, to fire me man to man. You drag in this third party. Is an audience necessary? Somebody else has to be a part of the end of my career!"

His poise abruptly returned. "Pardon me?" Seymour asked with more force than he had let out in the entire conversation so far.

She finally spoke with an unexpectedly sweet and youthful voice. "I can leave if it bothers him that much," she said.

For a moment, Seymour shifted in his chair to face her. Then, he turned and glared at me. "Absolutely not. This son of a bitch is going to hell and I only wish that I had more friends here to watch this." A second passed, and Seymour smiled. "Get the fuck out of my office."

August 27, 2003

I wandered for a few hours. My anger slowly subsided after I got so fired up from yelling at Seymour.

Eventually, I wound up in a small karaoke bar. I racked my brain for a few extra moments in order to decide what I wanted to drink. "Long Island Iced Tea," I said.

As the bartender mixed my concoction together, I fiddled with the wallet in my pocket. After feeling the thick wad of bills in my pocket I added, "Keep them coming."

As I sped along to intoxication, the crowd grew, and soon the opening chords of a cheerful 70s pop song were a fleeting harbinger of the obscenity to follow. An aging woman, whose voice suggested she had consumed a bottle of tequila and a half-carton of cigarettes within the last three hours, turned a sweet and jubilant love song into a bitter diatribe. At first I was horrified, but decided her "upper middle-aged" venom suited my mood, and in my stupor, I demanded an encore. I grinned at her.

Her creepy reciprocal smile from across the room stifled my enthusiasm, but I was content to sit there all night and listen to her sing those beautiful lyrics with all that rage.

A few hours later, I finally decided to go home. After an extended struggle with the lock, I stumbled into my apartment blind drunk. My distended belly jiggled under my partially unbuttoned dress shirt. I leaned on end tables, a couch, the armoire, and door handles en route to my bed. I landed face first and smelled the dry sweat from the night before. I coughed violently and fell asleep as the spasm receded.

I dreamed of myself as a much younger man prancing along a Technicolor rainbow with my happy friends. At the end, I kissed my vivacious lover, and she ecstatically trembled in my strong tanned arms.

I awoke and spewed across the bed. My head throbbed from a hangover and congested sinuses. It was still dark.

I cleaned the bed and disinfected it with ferocious speed. "Cleanliness is next to godliness," my mother preached when I did chores as a child. I cut a few lines of cocaine and went to the bathroom for a shot of vodka.

I stood before the mirror in the yellow-tiled bathroom but refused to reflect upon the image. The alarm clock in the next room went off while I stood there. When it stopped, I clenched my teeth. "It's show time!" I growled sarcastically.

(Thursday afternoon)

I flicked my new MetroCard as the train barreled into Manhattan. It was already well past noon, and I was in no hurry at all to reach the office for one final visit to clean out my office. I rode the train to Thirty-Fourth Street and, moments later, stood at an interesting crossroads. The normal path was up the stairwell, which exited in front of a big department store. For the first time, I noticed the corridor to the left. I walked up the slightly inclined path, and it led to the mall.

I went to the eighth-floor food court, and with a surprising amount of difficulty managed to procure my lunch. I walked toward the front the floor and eyed the tables by the floor to ceiling windows. I walked a little faster and got the last one in my line of sight that was available. I slumped my head down and started to eat. Moments later, as I was nearly finished with my enjoyment of a fast-food "entrée," I looked up.

Far ahead of me, another person emerged from the other side of the food court. This person was wearing gray-rimmed black sunglasses, and a lime green shirt. ***I will never get this wearing sunglasses indoor thing***, I thought to myself and looked back down of the remainder of my food.

Shortly afterward, approaching footsteps drew my attention. When I looked up, the footsteps stopped and the same young man stood before me. On his tray were a croissant and a bottle of ginger ale. "Can I help you?" I asked.

"I need a chair," he said. I held my hand out to offer it to him. He grabbed the chair and said, "I also need a table."

I laughed. "I am almost finished here," I said. "I don't mind sharing my table with you for two minutes."

"Two minutes," he remarked and sat down. "I guarantee you that I will prove so fascinating in the next two minutes that you will be riveted."

"Okay." I grinned. "We can start with names. My name is Barry Bowman."

"Barry Bowman. That would be fine alliteration if your middle name started with a B as well."

I grasped my neck with my left hand to shield my embarrassment. "My parents were a pretty nutty pair, um . . . what's your name?" I asked.

"Your middle name first," he said forcefully.

"Bernard."

"Barry Bernard Bowman. It's nice to meet you. I'm Yost Trenko."

"What the fuck," I remarked, completely not comprehending.

"Yost. Y-O-S-T. That's my first name. Trenko. T-R-E-N-K-O. That's my last name."

"Yost Trenko."

"Stellar pronunciation. Obviously it's not my real name."

"You'd almost think it were an acronym or anagram," I said curiously.

"That would be clever. By the way, what is a suit doing in the mall at maybe . . ." He leaned forward, eyed my watch, and continued, "Two thirty in the afternoon? Late lunch?"

"Hardly. How about you?"

"I'm waiting for a friend. How about you?"

I paused for a few seconds as I tried to think of a way to change the subject. "What's the deal with lunch?" I asked nervously.

"I'm not too hungry," he said, giving me a calculating look. "How about you?"

"I got fired yesterday." He nodded. "I change the subject when I'm nervous," I added.

"I got fired once. Last summer I worked for a credit card company. It was frustrating because I could not give out credit card numbers over the phone under any circumstances. One time this guy was determined to get the number from me. At one point, he asked, 'Does it start with a two?' I mean really, what do you say to that person?"

"Yes," I slyly suggested.

"Indeed!" Yost rapidly nodded his head and smiled.

"How old are you?"

"I'll be twenty-one in two weeks. And you?"

"I'm thirty," I said as though I was confessing a sin. "You still go to school?" I asked.

"Yes."

"Where?"

"I'd rather not say because if I were to tell you, then you would have expectations of me which are untrue."

"Every detail has a connotation."

"I love how you found the assumption underlying my argument, Barry. Maybe you're not such a dumb ass after all. What do you do?"

"Every detail has a connotation," I said grimly.

From the Journal of Yost Trenko

August 27, 2003

Janine e-mailed me the last chapter of Jed's story this morning. Jed wanted to meet with me so we could discuss it. I did read it. It was terrible, but I didn't want to make him feel bad. I considered lying to him, but if he's decided that he doesn't want to write any more, there is no reason to be honest. Barry Bernard Bowman (hereafter, BBB) could write something more compelling than the final chapter of Jed's brief crap-sterpiece.

BBB is going to kill himself. He's a suit who got fired and doesn't know what to do. Wah Wah Wah. Maybe he'll do more coke now. I chatted with him at the eighth-floor food court in the mall on Thirty-Fourth before Jed arrived. He got me so depressed that I decided to lie and give Jed a great review. If I didn't, then both Jed and BBB would have wound up in the same morgue. These glum people are driving me batty.

I've had no success yet. I work a shit job, and I've spent the last year rewriting the same chapter over and over. BBB and Jed Haele just ate shit for the first time in their charmed lives. They expect sympathy from me?

Jed wants to give up. "I've got to get away," he said glumly. He wore tight jeans and a thin white leather jacket. Throughout our conversation, he eyed my ginger ale longingly, since he doesn't eat sugar anymore.

"From what? The city?"

"You're right. That's it. I must withdraw, and that can't be a passive act. Passive withdrawal never takes. Withdrawal must be . . . ferocious."

Oy vey! He went on and on like that. Maybe he'll call his next novel ***Ferocity in Withdrawal.*** The kids will love it!

I gave him my golden review. "That ending was fucking brilliant, man!"

He smiled a little. "You sure?" he asked timidly.

"Oh, absolutely," I said. "You left me wanting more." Translation: "Your story was toothless and left me wanting an actual story."

"Thanks, dude. I appreciate it," he said. Then, he checked his hair in the window, stood up, and swaggered away. What a tool!

From the Journal of Jed Haele

August 27, 2003

Yost convinced me to stay in New York. He loved the chapter, and I trust him because he's a writer.

That leaves me with two options: Dad's job or writing. I could attempt to do both, but I suspect a full-time office job will require more of my time than managing a sandwich shop.

I cannot go to Virginia. I need to let Juliana Banyon down gently.

(Later)

Juliana arrived at my apartment earlier tonight without any advance warning. She was so angry. "All you do is throw shit way! I know that you're not going back with me. I never expected it, but how can you ignore me for three days like this. I'm on vacation!"

I intended to call her. I swear. My entry from earlier today is evidence! Besides, Juliana did say that she and Cheyenne were on vacation. I gave them space to enjoy their vacation.

I stood by the window. "I'm sorry. I didn't mean to ruin your vacation."

"You did. I'm . . ." She trailed off. Then, she ran her left hand through her hair and looked away from me.

"Not that kind of girl," I suggested.

She nodded. "I'm not a prude, but your lifestyle is too much. Your friends!"

"Yeah, but I've enjoyed this life."

In the end, Juliana made my choice even easier. I can't leave New York, but I will miss her.

From the Journal of Juliana Banyon

August 27, 2003

I paced around our suite all night long, again. I guzzled a few bottles from the mini bar. My hands trembled, and I spilled some of the last bottle on my shirt. I stewed in the corner of our twenty-third-floor window as the sun rose, while Cheyenne slept so soundly on her bed.

She woke up and saw the growing bags under my eyes from another night without sleep, surely smelling the whiskey. "You need to confront him. This is so shitty," she said. I nodded. I went to my bed and slept until three. I got dressed and went to his apartment.

I yelled at him. Then, he made an "apology" and sat down beside me. I could not look him in the eye.

"I've enjoyed this life, but you are right, Juliana." He sat on the black leather sofa next to me. "I could go with you and leave all this torment behind. You do know what happened here, right?" I shook my head. "The murder."

I turned to face him. "Murder," I whispered.

"My best friend was killed here." I stood up. "I can still smell it. It's weaker now, but that horrid butcher shop stench is still here," he added.

"You didn't tell me about this. Why do you think that you told me?" I was sincerely puzzled.

He frowned. "I thought that I told you."

"You did not tell me."

"Well, that happens to me sometimes. I'll think I have told somebody something, and later discover that I didn't." He paused. "I started a normal journal shortly after he was murdered. I kept a different kind of journal when I was a writer. My emphasis was always on writing. I wrote about writing. I explained my thought processes for all of the books, even the last one. Then Dean was murdered, and that mode of writing suddenly felt so inappropriate."

"When did it happen?"

"August 4. That's when I closed the book on my 'journal/literary exercises' and began to keep a journal. That day when I met you was the first time I felt well enough to leave my apartment. The hate kept me here."

"What?"

"The hatred. Shane believed that I was a destroyer, and his hate kept me here. It forced me to think about my life in a place haunted by his hatred. I now realize that I have to contain my evil." He glared at me and suddenly turned pale. "That's why I need to stay here. I can't pollute you and Cheyenne. There is only one place for me."

"You need to leave now, Juliana," he said in a chilly monotone. He stood up and walked across the room to his bedroom door. "I suddenly feel ill."

"What's wrong?"

He was sweating now and looked more feverish with each passing second, but stood alarmingly still. "Nothing that concerns you. Kindly leave my apartment now, Juliana," he said louder.

It was a very bizarre encounter, and Jed clearly has not recovered from the murder. I hope he seeks out psychiatric help soon, because I think that he was undergoing some sort of breakdown or panic attack when I left him. It was somewhat contagious because my heart started to beat faster, and I felt a bit nauseous.

From the Journal of Justin Simonds

August 29, 2003

It was a slow Friday afternoon at work before the two detectives arrived. They spoke with my gimp supervisor for a few minutes, and then he directed them to me. One of them had a grungy overgrown mustache. The other one was clean-cut, tall, and skinny.

The guy with the soup catcher lip fur did most of the talking. "I'm Detective Pinette, and this is my partner Detective Grace. We have some questions for you regarding Shane Lasch. Your supervisor has informed us that you were friends with Mr. Lasch when he worked here. Is this correct?"

"Yes, though I haven't heard from him in a few weeks." I pulled up my e-mail, and searched for his last message. "I'm looking for the last . . ."

"Do you know where he is?" Pinette asked.

"That's what I'm looking for. He told me that he was moving away." I glanced up from my monitor for a moment. The silent detective frowned.

"What?" I asked.

"We have had a very difficult time. Mr. Lasch has some annoying friends. Present company excluded, so far."

"I guess so. That's right." I laughed. "Okay. Here goes. I have enjoyed being friends, blah blah. I will move to San Diego next week. I will e-mail you. Yeah. He promised to e-mail me the new address, but he never did it. I haven't heard from him since this e-mail from July 31. Anything else?"

"That's most of it," Pinette said. "What can you say about his acquaintance with Jed Heely?"

"Jed Haele? The writer?" He nodded. "Shane told me a story that mimicked Jed's last release a couple of weeks before Jed distributed it. Shane claimed that he saw a telepathic serial killer in action. Shane seemed a bit delusional, so I didn't take it too seriously. When I read Jed's story, I was very confused. That was the last time that I tried to contact Shane. I sent him the story, and then he sent me this e-mail. The similarities shocked me at first, but Jed's story deviated from Shane's in the subsequent chapters, so I ultimately assumed that it was a coincidence. I mean, an evil telepathic is not that original of a subject for horror fiction."

"Horror fiction?"

"Yeah. That's how I would classify Jed. He was a horror novelist." I paused. "I didn't answer your other question. When I read the chapter and had déjà vu, I thought that there was a chance that he knew Jed and believed that he was the destroyer, but the last two chapters—"

Detective Grace abruptly cut me off. "Destroyer," he said very loud.

Pinette patted his back a few times. "That's a very big deal, Justin."

"In the story, that's the word his character used," I said.

"That's the word that Shane used in the very disturbing letter he composed while he waited for Jed to come home the day of the murder. He believed that Jed was a destroyer and intended to kill him, but he screwed up and killed Jed's friend instead."

"The murder? I guess that's why Shane moved so far away and didn't give his friends too many details."

Pinette scoffed, and Grace scowled at me. "This destroyer concept is . . ."

Okay. I can't write any more of this. Those detectives gave me the creeps. It degenerated into this odd sort of lecture where they went on and on with this ominous talk about destroyers. It seemed straightforward enough to me. Shane was deluded. He killed somebody. It's not the first time that a crazy person tried to murder the subject of their delusions. That said, I guess he really did run into Jed Haele all those times. That's kind of weird.

From the Journal of James Pinette

August 29, 2003

It doesn't make any sense. I don't understand how a person with no history of mental illness can just turn like that. I read the kid's file cover to cover. He was 100 percent normal until three months ago. Yeah, there was the family thing, but he handled it okay, even though his aunt said he got bratty and drank more recently. He's been dealing with that for a while. He was a trooper, and then he met Jed Haele and went off the deep end. Jed was stupid enough to write the book about this craziness that came out of nowhere, and then it degenerated into murder. It's all so abrupt that the only reasonable explanation is that Jed really is this telepathic destroyer, and he somehow fucked up Shane's brain. That's a problem, because I don't handle supernatural criminal activity. Well, it's not my problem anymore. It should be easy for them to track him down in San Diego, with his mangled hand and all. Shane will be in an asylum for decades. Maybe they will figure it out.

I don't like this Jed kid at all. Why was he living with that faggot? Why didn't he take more precautions? He saw Shane mutilate himself! Personally, I think Jed is the bigger question mark.

My stomach is burning. I feel like I am going to cough up blood. This heartburn is terrible.

Another day, another dollar. Another day, another dollar. Another day, another dollar. That's my mantra. "Mantra" is my swell new word of the day!

From the Journal of Jed Haele

August 29, 2003

I printed all of my texts this morning and made a pile on my bed. I laid down beside the pile and pulled it close. I ran the plot of ***Dance of the Damned*** through my brain, as if it were a pitch, and realized that it was a ridiculous novel.

I called Dad and said yes. This choice has been too easy.

August 31, 2003

The detective called me last night.

"Mr. Heely?"

"It is pronounced 'Hale,' remember?"

"Yes. That's right. Well, Mr. Haele, we have some good news for you. Shane Lasch is now in custody. He was apprehended in San Diego last night."

"Oh. That's great to hear."

"That's all?" he cackled softly, then coughed into the phone. "I was expecting some more relief than that." "Oh, no. I've taken precautions. I haven't worried about Shane at all. How's his hand?"

"Mr. Lasch is not in good shape. He's totally batshit now."

The detective informed me of Shane's location, and I advised him that I intended to visit him in jail.

"I wasn't expecting that." He paused, resuming with a softer tone. "I shouldn't be telling you this, but he has been asking about you. He's made accusations, but nobody's taking him seriously. The insanity defense should be real easy for his attorney."

"What kind of accusations?"

"He said that you broke his hand. Don't worry about it. The police report from the incident on June 14 is very clear. Good day, Mr. Haele."

I'm not surprised. I knew that they would get him, since Shane is not too smart. It's almost amusing that he's still the same kind of crazy.

From the Journal of Yost Trenko

September 2, 2003

I registered for the fiction novel workshop at school, per Jed's suggestion. I went to the first class today. Dr. Grayson arrived late, dropped into his seat, and began lecturing without so much as a good afternoon. I taped him, so what follows is my verbatim transcript: "You are fiction novelists this semester. You are not writing short fiction. You are not poets, screenwriters, or journalists in this class. This semester, you will write in the most prominent literary format of the last two centuries. You will all try to write a novel." He paused and stared at us very sternly. "You are about to compose an abortion. That is my only guarantee, because that is the only level of success a room full of twenty-year-olds can hope to accomplish in three months. Get out of here, start writing, and come back next week with a chapter. E-mail it to me, and e-mail it to everyone else. Next week, I will explain to each of you why you have failed. Have a good afternoon."

Clearly, Mr. Grayson is the type of person who rips his bandages off in one fast swipe. I love him already.

I think that I will hand in the first chapter of "Nunqum Fidelis," which is a novel about mercenary free agents set in a dystopian future on the West Coast. I'll work on chapter two this week and submit it the following week. Thus, I will be a chapter ahead of the class each week for the entire semester!

From the Journal of Jed Haele

September 2, 2003

I took a very early flight. I rapidly drank two small bottles of white wine and got nearly five hours of sleep.

I had a strange dream, where I was the stationary observer of astral phenomena. Autumnal colors mostly illuminated that segment of space, but there were also blotches of purple and pink. I stared at the grim brown and orange hues while a grinding pulse played in the background. It got cold, and I convinced myself that I was staring at billions of dead souls, and that all the strangely colored space dust represented them.

This transitioned to a cold and dirty apartment where a sickly bald woman cowered near a cheap heater. She looked up but didn't see me. The neon-orange coils illuminated her small face. I was physically unable to speak. I tried, but my throat tightened. She turned around and crawled to the window. She had black lesions on her neck and scalp. I walked into her kitchen. The refrigerator was partially open, and the light was off. There was a newspaper on the dirty white table. The date on the page was July 17, 1987. I looked ahead, and the clock by the window read 7:06.

I woke up in sunny San Diego and was safely back in the twenty-first century. I held my hand in my pocket and felt the paper with the address of the jail. I walked through the airport slowly. When I got to the sprawling baggage claim area, it seemed even brighter. So many people were smiling, and I joined in while I waited for my bags between two other travelers. "I'm here to visit a murderer," I said quietly to myself, grinning harder. "This airport is so clean," I said to the young female traveler on my left.

"It's lovely."

"Indeed."

"You're from New York?"

"Of course."

"Well, enjoy your time here. I love it." She giggled. "It's a great place to live." I nodded, and we continued to stare at the conveyor belt.

Once I acquired my bag, I got a cab. "The Camden Correctional Facility. It's in National City," I said to my young driver. He nodded, eyeballing me via the rearview mirror. "I'm visiting an old foe." He laughed. "Yeah. It's like that."

"Have you ever been to a jail before?" he asked. He had an Irish accent.

"Nope."

"It's not so bad, if you're just visiting."

"Yep. I'm just visiting."

We didn't chat for the rest of the ride. It went fast. The city looked very different from years ago. There were many new buildings in the Gaslamp District. It was unrecognizable. I hadn't been to the city since 1994.

Then, he pulled up to a drab off-white building. "I won't be long, so you can let the meter run and hold my bag."

"Sure," he said. Then, he turned around and added, "Watch out for yourself."

"It will be fine."

He tapped his head with his forefinger. "Watch out for you mind, friend. Didn't you ever see ***The Silence of the Lambs***?"

"I understand," I said soberly.

I walked inside fast, and the attendant directed me to go to the fifth floor.

I met Carlos there, who led me to the visitor area. Carlos was quite pleasant. He patted my shoulder a few times and tried to make small talk. I didn't expect that.

Once we reached the chilly room, I took a seat at the table and waited for Shane. "Oh shit, his hand!" I said to myself. I was suddenly quite anxious to see the progress.

Carlos wheeled him into the room. His legs were tied to the chair, and the good arm was cuffed to the chair. His free stub hung limply over the other arm, with an orange muff over the end. His eyes were glazed over. "Is this my visitor?" he asked Carlos. Carlos nodded, pushed him to the table, and backed away. Shane leaned forward and stared at me.

"Hello, Shane. It's Jed."

His mind and eyes processed my words and my image slowly at first. He continued to stare at me.

Suddenly, he lurched back up in his chair, and his eyes grew wide with fear. "No! No! Please!" he yelled. "Carlos. Fuck! Oh God! Please don't leave me here!" He shook his body in the chair and tried to turn it so that he could kick himself away, but the chair flipped over and fell on his bad arm. The bar was wedged over his stump. Carlos leaned down and tried to pick up the chair, but Shane didn't stop shaking.

When Carlos finally got his chair back up, the muff was dripping with blood. Carlos ran to the door and screamed for the medic. With his head turned to Carlos, Shane screamed at the absolute top of his lungs. "GET ME AWAY FROM THE DESTROYER!" His chest heaved hard. He took a few more deep panic breaths and screamed the same sentence again with a rasp. Carlos returned and grabbed the chair.

"Hold it!" I said forcefully.

"But he—," Carlos said.

I cut him off. "They'll be here soon," I said to him. I leaned forward. "Shane! Shane! Shane! Look at me now. No! No! Turn around," I said desperately. "I'm not going to hurt you with my mind. I promise." Carlos frowned at me, and I shook my hand at him. Shane continued to whimper, but slowly turned his head around to face me. "I'm not going to hurt you," I said softly. "I told you that. There you go. Okay, that's good." I stared straight in his eyes. "I forgive you, Shane. I had to come here so I could tell you that. Do you understand?"

He shook his head. "You don't know that you are a Destroyer." He raised the bloody stump to his face. "It's subconscious, Jed. You have no choice, but they are your deeds." He shook his head more violently, and Carlos wheeled him out of the room.

September 3, 2003

I just re-read what I wrote yesterday, and I don't buy it. I don't forgive Shane, and I don't know why I said that to him.

Rather, my apparent good deed did not go unpunished. I went right back to the airport and took the red-eye last night. I didn't sleep on the plane, because I couldn't get the new dimension of his allegations out of my head. He could be correct. It's very unlikely, but this model of my "powers" is a possibility, and that's disturbing. If I had powers and wasn't conscious of them, I could go my entire life ignorant of those deeds.

It's also disturbing to come home to the airport and not have a friend waiting there for you. When I went on vacations in the past, Dean usually met me at the airport when I got home. This was yet another sad reminder of how my life is so different now.

Getting back to Shane's speculation, I do want to conclude that I don't believe in this new notion at all. Rather, I find it fascinating, as it does eclipse the fictional model that I tried to create. It is odd that there is a person in the world who thinks of me that way, but it is a fiction. I have faith in that fact.

September 19, 2003

It's been two weeks, and all I've done since is hock heart attacks in aluminum foil wrappers for drones.

It's Friday night, but I don't have the gumption to get out. To be honest, I am not even motivated to write in this journal. I am so tired.

October 27, 2003

I had terrible insomnia tonight. I usually have trouble getting to sleep on Sunday nights, but tonight was very difficult. I'm writing an entry because I have nothing better to do.

I was thinking about something that a producer said to me at a premiere a few months ago. He said his motto was "With bitterness and rage, I proceed." I thought it was very creepy at the time, but I understand now.

I pursue my goals with bitterness and rage every Monday morning. It's colder now. When I leave, it's dark. I ride the train and hope for delays so I can have an extra ten minutes to read my magazine.

January 19, 2004

It's been a long time. I'm not writing fiction anymore, so I don't need to keep a journal.

I paused over that last sentence to reflect upon the fucked-up logic.

The last four months proceeded exactly as expected. I went back to work at the Sterling Subs. I paid my dues for four months, and then Dad gave me the "keys" to work at his office.

I've been in the office for almost three weeks now. The job is not exciting at all, but I don't care. I am a well-compensated cog. In addition, I finally met my dad's mistress.

Kate is a well-preserved forty-year-old red-headed überfrau. She's perfectly groomed, and I don't think that she has worn a wrinkled shirt in her entire life.

I don't have a life or friends any more. In addition, everybody in the office hates me because of the nepotism. Of course, they aren't open about it, but I can smell their resentment.

The worst part is I see my dad every day. On the bright side I haven't seen my mom in weeks. The last time I saw her was Christmas Day. She went on another vacation last week, but I cannot remember the destination.

Enough for today. I just don't have the energy for this. Compared to the sandwich shop, this job entails more hours and more work. I'm exhausted at the end of the day. I don't have time to go to the gym or clubs any more.

January 21, 2004

I didn't expect to write again so soon. The journal was a utilitarian exercise when I was a writer. It would be a chore now. What's the point?

Well, there is a point. I want to resume. I always enjoyed keeping a regular journal. I've missed it. In addition, I have something to write about today.

I slept with Kate! I just got home from her apartment. It's the twenty-second now, but anyway, here's how it went down on the twenty-first.

I've suspected that she was attracted to me since the day I met her. After all, I have a strong resemblance to my dad, but I'm thirty-five years younger. I think she wants to work both ends against the middle. Since Dad is not very healthy, she figures that I will inherit the power.

She invited me to lunch yesterday via e-mail. I accepted, and we went to a small Mediterranean restaurant, which was on a side street between Fifth and Sixth Avenue. The food was strange. We got vodka martinis (an acceptable midday drink for any business professional) and flirted while I picked at a grimy pesto dish.

"I need to buy shit for my apartment," I said. "Now that I'm making so much money."

"You'd like my apartment. I just bought all this cool Shaker furniture. It juxtaposes nicely with my edgy art collection," she said and followed it with more mouthfuls about her art collection. I tuned out and focused on her thin, but sensual lips.

That's all it took. She "wink, wink" invited me to come over and check out her apartment after work. I checked it all out. I checked her inside out! I have never seen a better body on a woman her age. I guess the vegan food works.

From the Journal of Kate

January 3, 2004

Well, Seymour's kid finally arrived, and HE IS HOT. I feel like a teenager again, and I am definitely going to sleep with him. I'll wait a few weeks, but I will do it. He looks like a model; a brunette male model with the best ass. I bet he can thrust it.

January 18, 2004

I was bored today, so I did some calculations and got very depressed. I received the paycheck with my year-end bonus. The gross amount of my bonus was $17,500, and I cleared $9,000. I cannot emotionally cope with that.

I slink around that joint like a composed robot lady, eat shit from the people who hate me because I am fucking the boss, lust after my boss/fuck buddy's son, get dolled up to perfection, and get up at 6:30 a.m. every day to enjoy it six days a week. $9,000 is inadequate compensation. I am forty years old. This can't be my life.

January 21, 2004

I fucked Jed, and it was damn fucking weird.

Okay. Here's what happened. We went to lunch yesterday, and I flirted very aggressively with him over vegan food. I told him about my cool apartment and invited him to come. (Yuck. Yuck.)

We went after work today. I made drinks while he looked over my art collection. He settled on my couch and had a weird glow in his eyes when I returned. He refused the drinks and got to it quite aggressively. He stood up, stripped, and forcefully helped me strip too. Pushing me down on the couch, he slid down over me. His body pulsed. It was a mild vibration that I attributed to an elevated heart rate. In retrospect, I'd say it was a rather abnormal sensation. His eyes bugged out also. It was freaky. He quickly covered my face with his cold hands, and I felt a slight static electric shock when they made impact.

Regardless, it was a great forceful fuck. I had a nosebleed afterward! In addition, he's bigger than his dad is and lasts much longer.

From the Journal of Jed Haele

January 22, 2004

I got a call from Janine today. I was in the middle of a Sterling Sub when I saw the old familiar number on my caller ID. She had graduated from school one semester ahead of schedule. I congratulated her and offered to treat her to lunch on Sunday. "Let's go to the Banyon's in Chelsea," she suggested.

"That's a great choice. It's quiet. We can catch up." In other news, Kate didn't show up for work today, so I dodged that bullet. I was in no mood for awkward moments like ***that***.

From the Journal of Seymour Haele

January 23, 2004

Kate died from a massive aneurysm in her sleep Wednesday night. Her mother called me at the office to give me the news today. I announced it to the office, and nobody cried or even looked sad. I guess those fuckers knew about us. Oh well.

With Fiona off in Nepal, I have no one to fuck, so I have a whole lot of masturbation to cover. I guess I need to buy porn tomorrow.

Or now?

From the Journal of Jed Haele

January 24, 2004

I arrived early and ordered a dry vodka martini at the bar. The restaurant was empty and smelled funky. Janine called me. "I'm going to be late, Jed. I'll be there by four."

"Why?"

"I slept late and I have errands to do. Is it a problem?"

I did not want to wait two hours for her. "Well, that means I don't have anything to do for a while. I'm by myself."

"Aren't you used to this now?"

I laughed. "Yeah. You're right. I think I can handle it. I'll be at the bar."

I finished my drink and then took a walk along Twenty-third Street. It was overcast. I headed for the Flatiron Building. I couldn't believe another autumn and another holiday season had passed so fast. I'd been in that office so much recently.

"Where is Gramercy Park?" I asked myself. "I should know where that is." I lazily searched for it, returning later to Banyon's.

When I got there, Janine was already at the bar. She was dressed very casually, looking like a teenager and drinking a mixed drink. "Jed Haele. It has been too long," Janine called when she saw me. She stood up and hugged me.

"Yes, it has," I added. "I don't have anything for you to type."

She smiled. "Let's get a table."

They sat us in a booth toward the back of the dark restaurant. "Why are so many restaurants in the city poorly lit?" I asked.

"This is news?" she asked huskily.

"It's taken me too long to make the observation," I said. She shrugged, and we proceeded to peruse the menu.

"I don't want steak," she whined.

"They have seafood. You want lobster tails? I've had them before, and they're good. I'll treat."

After too much deliberation, and visits from an impatient waiter, we finally ordered.

"Congratulations," I said abruptly. "Did you get a job yet?"

"Nope."

"Do you miss typing up my stories?" I asked.

She puckered in her cheeks and shrugged.

"I don't miss writing them," I added.

She stared at me for a few seconds. "You will."

I leaned back in my seat. "Never," I said. "It was hell at the end. Absolute hell."

"What's your life like now?"

"Ah, yes. I remember this. The hard questions. You always challenge me with hard questions. I've missed that part of our relationship."

"You bring that out of me. I don't know why."

We split an order of bacon-wrapped shrimp. They weren't very good, but we ate them fast nonetheless. "They're so dry," I said.

"Yes, they are."

"So, what's next?"

"I don't know."

"How does that feel?"

"It's a good feeling. I'll keep it going for a while."

"As long as you can."

"Yeah." She looked at the empty plate. "I didn't call you so we could talk about me."

"Then what's the agenda, babe?" I asked sarcastically and immediately regretted my choice of words and tone of voice.

"I called because I have strong feelings about the choice you've made." She paused, but I gestured to her to go on. "You are squandering your talent by committing to this nine-to-five bullshit. I'm sorry, but I need to tell you this. My conscience hasn't been clear lately."

"I wrote shit, Janine."

"Yes. You're right, but I know that you could do better. I've always had faith in that, but I never thought you would be a quitter. You surprised me."

"I'm sorry, but I made my decision."

"You're going to regret it." She spoke faster. "You will. One day you're going to feel that regret, and that will be a very depressing day. It will be too late, and you will hate yourself."

I smiled at her. "Everybody eats shit, Janine. I've made all my own decisions, and I can live with that."

This back and forth continued throughout the rest of the meal. Neither of us backed down at all.

When we left, it was dark and icy sleet was falling. An inch of slush had accumulated on the ground. We stood in the doorway, both of us dreading the bitter winter weather. "This is gross," I said.

"Yeah. Did you see Howard Dean this week?"

I opened the door and went outside. "Okay. That was good. You helped me think of something more painful than this." I gestured at the precipitation that fell around me. "I have a scream! I have a scream!"

Then, she ventured past the threshold. "Yee-haw! Yee-haw!" she howled. She slipped and fell into my arms. We both laughed. I held her there, and she said, "This is weird."

"And so wrong," I added. She looked above me at the falling ice. "It's horrid, but it is sort of beautiful. The ice." The wind picked up and blew the crystals in her face. I gently brushed them away with my hand.

From the Journal of Chester Syme

January 25, 2004

Jed Haele's decision to end his writing career disappointed me greatly. His last novel was shoddy and incomplete. I moved on with my life, because there were better things to do. I did this with the hope that he would change his mind and resume his career.

One thing that I could not do was continue this journal. My last entry was for February 9, 2003! That's a long gap, but I've never had the patience to keep a journal on a daily basis. It's difficult, because you have to make too many choices. You have to choose the most salient points from your day and describe them as fully as possible.

My days are generally quite boring. I did get a job after college, and it is certainly not salient enough of a point to warrant any description here.

From the Journal of Roger Venable

January 25, 2004

The thing about Chester that's so unnerving is his monotone. He's so poised. It's inhuman.

For example, Jade and I had a huge fight over a late dinner at Jake Banyon's Steakhouse tonight. She kept slapping me. Chester and his fiancée sat opposite us, and he interjected after I banged my fist on the table. "That's unnecessary, Roger. She's just . . ." He paused to think and arched his head to crack his neck. "Asserting herself." He smiled. "Your relationship is at an early stage, and you need to develop your boundaries. That's the reason why Selena and I get along so swell. We only argue about serious things. We don't sweat the small stuff, right? Dear?" He turned and grinned at her. She reciprocated with even more enthusiasm.

I don't intend to get past the "early stage" with Jade. All I want to do is beat the shit out of her. It's difficult to resist that impulse, since she slaps me so much. We can't all be perfect like Chester, right?

From the Journal of Chester Syme

January 26, 2004

Today was unusual. It was a day full of salient points.

I have had very much patience with regard to Jed's decision. I assumed that he would change his mind and return to his fiction world. I have craved for more of this world. It's been so hard. All I have are those two books and that final incomplete novel. That last one was wretched. I know that it was marred by the murder of Dean Bazth by that crazy person. Jed lost focus. I understood that and accepted it, but I was so sad.

Anyway, let's get to the salient points.

First, I woke up this morning and shaved my head and eyebrows. I was concerned that my bald scalp might look weird, but it was pristine and white. There were no scars.

Second, I went to a department store and bought an off-white wet suit. They only had a few in stock, and they were marked down by 75 percent. While the fussbudget employee handled my purchase, some kids approached us and asked for the price of the premium chocolate bars that a small display case by his register housed. They were three dollars. The kids groaned and walked away. "They're not Hershey bars," he said with a British accent and scoffed. I smiled in agreement.

I went home and prepared for my outing. I put the necessary items in a small bag and put on the wet suit.

I arrived at Jed's apartment a half-hour past his usual arrival time from work. I stood by the door and put my ear up against it. He was alone. He was talking to himself and nobody reciprocated.

I opened my bag and pulled out my key. I opened the door, and Jed was understandably surprised. "What the fuck!" he yelled. Fortunately, I've got about fifty pounds and five inches of height over him. I punched him in the jaw and he fell down.

He passed out for a few minutes. While he was unconscious, I picked him up and sat him at his dining table. I pulled the skinny ropes out of my bag and tied up his feet. Then I tied his left hand and torso to the back of the chair, because I wanted to leave his right arm free.

When he came to and saw me, he screamed. I pulled the syringe out of my bag. "If you don't stop screaming, then I will inject you with this syringe."

"What's in it?"

"You don't want to know, Jed." He tried to kick his legs and attempted to undo the knots in the back with his right arm. "Please stop that." I held up the syringe again for emphasis and he ceased.

"How do you know my name?" he asked weakly.

"Yes, that's a good way to start." I pulled another chair away from the table and sat down. "I am a subscriber, and I have been very patient with you, Jed. I watched over you as you struggled with that third novel. I subscribed to that thing you released last year, about the destroyer. Then, without any warning whatsoever, you stopped." I took a deep breath and exhaled hard. "My patience has reached its limit. I'm here to punish you, Jed."

Of course, he started to scream again. I shook my head. I pulled the duct tape out of my bag and tore a piece off. I stood up and approached from the left side so his other arm wasn't in the way. He tried to use the free arm, but I swatted that skinny thing aside with my elbow and placed the tape over his mouth.

I stood back, and then he ripped it off with his free hand. He glared at me. I shook my head, and he screamed even louder. "I am going to put another piece on, Jed! If you take it off, I will tie up your other arm!"

"You can't do this to me!" he said, among other things. I don't have the patience to remember or transcribe any more of that whining.

"Shut up!" I yelled. I pointed the syringe in his direction with a stabbing motion, and he complied. At this point, I decided that it was not necessary to tape his mouth. "That's better. If you can keep the volume at a respectable level, then I won't have to gag you again." He nodded and then cried. "Okay. The punishment. I understand your feelings, Jed. I really do."

"Why are you doing this?"

"Well, I didn't tie your right hand down. Maybe that's a better question," I suggested.

"Why is my arm free?" He asked.

"It will remain free. It is the only appendage of yours that will ever be free again. Your other limbs are tied down, and you understand that I will not allow you to scream." Thankfully, he nodded. "I am going to provide you with paper, pen, and a few hours to write. You can do whatever you want with the time. You can write a suicide note," I suggested. "Maybe a short story. Maybe you can write one last journal entry. It would be a long one, but that's nothing new to you, is it? I am giving you a final opportunity to express yourself. That's the reason why I shaved my head and eyebrows and wore a wet suit. There should be no DNA trail in your apartment when I leave. I will do my best to ensure that." Of course, this was also for my protection. In addition, I never told him my name. "Thus, you can put any spin on this that you want. You will die, but I am giving you an option that most murder victims never receive. Dean didn't get this opportunity. You will." He shuddered and whimpered. I pulled my chair closer to him and sat down. I put the syringe back in my bag while I spoke. "So many people face imminent death without any option to express themselves. If you were to die in a car wreck tomorrow, you wouldn't get this opportunity. You would be gone in an instant, with no chance to reflect." A strand of snot dripped from his nose, and the tears kept dropping off his chin. "I'm sorry if this is no consolation, Jed, but you made this very difficult for me too. I'm sorry." I sighed hard. "Anyhoo, we need to get busy."

I grabbed a yellow legal pad from his desk and a pen. "Let's say three hours, Jed. It's a ballpark figure. If you need more time, I may be reasonable."

Instead of writing, he wanted to talk more. Since he kept the volume down and didn't try any more funny stuff, I obliged him. He wanted to know how I learned so much about him.

He's really smart. He read between the lines and gathered that I'd been stalking him. "Every step you take!" I cackled. "I've seen it all, Jed!"

He turned his head slowly and grinned at me angrily. "If I get the upper hand here and we switch our roles, I will force YOU to write about that reversal of fortune." He nodded. "Imagine yourself tied to this chair with a deadline. Yes!" He cocked his head. "I'll see you on the flip side." He paused, held up his free arm, and made a crude gesture. "Then I will kill you with your own mystery syringe. What do you think about that?"

"I think that's unlikely, Jed."

"We'll see about that, buddy boy." He dropped his arm back down and rested it on the table. He concentrated hard for a few moments and then started to write. He paused after every couple of words and seemed much calmer. After a while, I walked over to observe him closer. I stared down at the page.

Then, he lunged at my neck with the free arm. He held the pen between his thumb and forefinger, and tried to stab me in the neck with it while he grasped my throat with the other three fingers. He might have succeeded if he let the stabbing thing drop (he had a good hold on my neck), but his multitasking, or rather multi-pronged, mode of attack was his downfall. I swiftly pulled his arm off with my free appendages and went right for my syringe. I went to the couch and pulled it back out of my bag.

I returned to him. I held the syringe in my left hand and held down his free arm with my strong right hand. I leaned over his shoulder to see his face. His eyes bugged out and he glared at me hard, but a scintilla of fear came through as well. "You are a writer, correct?" His entire body trembled, and the chair vibrated slightly. "Well, here's a new word for you: disintegral. It's a word I invented. I'll define it. It's an adjective that describes an object whose disintegration is inevitable. For example, an ice sculpture is disintegral. Like you, it is poised to melt away for all time."

Epilogue
The Gordian Knots

From the Journal of Yost Trenko

January 25, 2004

Dr. Grayson gave me an "A" and it was the only one in the class. As if I was the best! I delivered an "abortion" just like the rest of my class, but I got the "A." Oh yeah! I also killed the curve in my investment finance class. I got the only "A" in that class as well.

January 26, 2004

Jed Haele was murdered. It's a pretty big local news story because it was the second murder in that apartment in less than a year. It's a different murderer, because the guy who killed Dean is in jail in California. The cops have no clue, and I don't either.

The cover of both prominent New York City tabloids had that small dark photo of Jed from ***Wired***, where he is naked with a laptop covering his crotch. It was a crass and insensitive photo to run, but they didn't have any choice. It was the only existing publicity photo of Jed Haele.

I called his ex-girlfriend about it, and she was inconsolable. Her moans were distorted and scratchy because of a bad connection. She said very bizarre self-destructive things. I'm a bit afraid for her. I don't think she is going to be well enough to go to the funeral on Wednesday.

From the Journal of Beatrice

January 26, 2004

All I want to do is cry. I think I am going to kill myself. I mean it this time.

Women used to do that when their men left them. Right? They withered away and died. Widows do that. I could do that.

(Later)

He wasn't my man. Makiko is my man, now.

(Later)

When I walk down the street, I am only attracted to women. Makiko and I wandered around Times Square yesterday. We went to the music store and split up for a while. I stared at a skinny blond teenage tourist's hips like I owned them. I discreetly followed her around the popular music aisles. Her fat friends trailed her, and they giggled at me.

I was ashamed of my sexuality for years. I fucked Jed and aborted two of his babies. I went to his house once and he wasn't there, so I gave his brother a blowjob. He was seventeen at the time.

I experimented with girls while Jed and I were exclusive but didn't get him involved with any of my "lesbian action." I'm sure he would have enjoyed it. My "friends" thought he was a fool, and I ***never*** defended him!

I've never done things like that to Makiko. I've been good to her, and I could handle her death. I wouldn't feel the same guilt, because I didn't betray her again and again and again.

(Later)

I lied before! I cheated on Makiko too. I'm a horrible and bitter person. I'm bitter because I won't have "the life" with Jed Haele now.

(Later)

Would I have gone back to him? Could I have become Mrs. Haele and had babies? What would Jed Jr. have looked like? Would we have grown old and established traditions?

Would I have hated myself every step of the way because of the fundamental dishonesty of the relationship?

From the Journal of Janine

January 26, 2004

I've never known anybody who died. Jed is my first, and I had a meal with him the day before he died. He was alive, and now he's dead. It's quite spooky. I've replayed that last conversation in my head. He was warm and ate with me on Saturday. The restaurant was hot, so he sweated a bit. He's cold and stiff now.

I can't fathom this. It's too sudden.

(Later)

He was murdered. They know nothing. The death scene was "very bizarre," according to the local tabloid, but the "cops did not specify any details" to reporters. I'll call his parents later.

January 27, 2004

I went to his parents' house. The last time I was there, I fucked a himbo in Jed's old room. His over-tanned dad answered the door and greeted me warmly. "Hello, dear. Please come in."

We walked through the chilly house. He led me to their huge living room in the back, which has floor-to-ceiling windows that overlook their pool. We sat on the white leather couch by the windows. "How did you know my son? I don't recall, um . . ." He trailed off and stared at me.

"Really?"

He nodded. "I lost track. Even though he worked for me, I saw very little of him the last few years. I rarely met any of his friends." He paused, and his eyes glazed over. "Even the last few weeks, when he worked in my office, I saw so little of him."

"I had lunch with him on Saturday."

He sighed. "So he didn't lose track of you."

"Oh, no. We did. I was his typist, but since he stopped . . ."

He cut me off. "That's right. You're Janine. I'm sorry. It's been quite disorienting, and I'm medicated right now."

I did not want him to elaborate, so I abruptly changed the subject. "How is Chester taking it?"

"He's away. He'll be at the funeral, but he is away today. It's been so strange here. The detectives call a few times a day because they are so clueless. They don't know what happened. There was no DNA evidence or any sign of a break-in to his apartment. Apparently, he was murdered by a phantom."

"How's Fiona handling it?"

"His mother?" He shook his head. "Unreachable."

"Where is she?"

"She's in Nepal."

"By herself?"

"Yes. She is doing much better now."

I did not ask him to elaborate again. He was so grim. "I'll be there, Seymour."

"That means a lot, Janine."

From the Journal of Makiko

January 28, 2004

Beatrice and I went to Jed's funeral today. It started at three, but Beatrice and I arrived early. The funeral home in Fresh Meadows was rather dark and dingy.

Beatrice has been wigging out since we got the news, and the only person that she could tolerate in Jed's family was his mom. She wasn't there. "Jed's mother is unreachable. She's on vacation in a remote region of Nepal," Jed's dad explained to me. "I've made dozens of calls to Kathmandu so far."

"Oh." I get along well with Jed's dad. A few of Jed's writer gatherings took place at his parents' house, and I had a number of fun conversations with Seymour when I got bored with some of the other writers (e.g., Yost).

"Check out that ass!" I said, as Beatrice slowly walked down the aisle to view the body. She wore a fitted black skirt. "Scrumptious!" I said and cackled with him.

"You're lucky. I just lost my piece of ass."

"That mistress? Shit!"

"Yeah. She died last week. Did I ever show you a picture?"

"Yeah. You finally got to fuck a Jewess."

"Mom would be so happy."

I cackled some more, and we went outside to share a joint. We leaned over his car in the parking lot. I lit it and took the first hit. "Man! Oh man!" I exhaled. "This is fucked up."

"Damn." He took it from me, took a deep drag, and held it for a long time. He leaned back against his Jaguar, stood straight as a rod, and a single tear dropped from his left eye as he slowly exhaled. "You want to hear a secret, Makiko."

"Sure."

"Jed's sold six thousand novels since he died."

I choked on my second hit of the joint. "Posthumous success?"

"Yeah. Gimme that again," he said grimly. "I am keeping it quiet until Fiona comes back. It's a private family matter, particularly due to the issues with his last book."

"I understand, Seymour."

The funeral director appeared in the lot. "Mr. Haele. You need to come inside."

I went with him. As we approached the door, we heard loud screams. The funeral director held the door for us, and we ran to the viewing room. Beatrice was slumped over the casket and yelled loudly. She pounded on his chest. "Baby. Stop it." I paced ahead of Seymour. I grabbed her arm to pull her up, and she yielded easier than I expected. Her eyes were red from fresh tears. "I smelled him. I smelled his cold chest, Makiko." She looked down at my hand and grabbed the joint. "I'm not going to make it through this, Makiko. I'm not going to survive," she said desperately and took a hard and fast puff, which burned the joint nearly down to her gray lips. "He who dances the dance of the damned," she mumbled with the rapidly disintegrating ember between her lips. It was barely intelligible, but I recognized the dialogue from Jed's novel. She spit it out and continued more clearly. "He who dances the dance of the damned never grasps the cold, bitter darkness of his wretched heart. He struts and twirls across that dank and chilly hall. Their blood pools to puddles, and he gaily splashes them. He does one last spin while they all die and never sheds a tear for them. It is the gate to hell."

That was a good spot to leave. We went home, she took her pills, and the rest of my evening was peaceful.

From the Journal of Beatrice

January 29, 2004

I had a placid dream last night. We were at the beach, about a mile from the Santa Monica Pier in Los Angeles. It was an overcast warm afternoon. We were wrapped in a blanket on the sand. He pulled off my amber sunglasses and kissed me with his soft lips. I tasted residue from Cherry Coke.

Suddenly, the sun started to set and everything was drenched with that gorgeous dirty pink light. He withdrew and stared at the choppy waves ahead of us. "I love you," I said.

When I woke up, Makiko sat by the window in her underwear. She was on the phone and smoking a joint. She laughed her chirpy laugh, and I covered my head with the blanket.

In the darkness, I breathed until the air turned heavy and warm. Then, I opened a small hole at the side, and some cool fresh air drifted inside.

It hurts really bad, but I need to live. I've squandered enough, and I cannot do this anymore. Jed would have wanted me to be strong, and I will honor his memory by doing so.

From the Journal of Janine

January 28, 2004

Yost drove me to the funeral in Queens this afternoon. It was a warm and overcast day for late January. The temperature has gone up a bit the last few days. The funeral and the burial were quite somber and quiet. We arrived late and quietly took seats near the back.

Jed's dad gave a boring speech about his accomplishments in school and his businesses and how Chester will have "big shoes to fill" as Jed's replacement. Yost quietly scoffed at Seymour's cliché, but I chose to be more charitable and maintain my grief-stricken composure.

The burial was similarly subdued, but the wake was quite different.

When Simon arrived, he made a beeline for Seymour, and within a few moments of conversation, Seymour started yelling at him. "You fucker!" Seymour yelled. That was the first line that caught my attention. Yost and I walked over, as they exchanged harsher words. "This is totally inappropriate, Simon!"

Simon glared at me as we approached. "Here she comes. Hey, Janine," he said. "It's Janine and w-what's his name? Another literary fucker. Toast?"

"It's Yost," he said.

"Yeah. That's right. Well, Yost, I was asking Seymour about novel sales since the murder. You do know that those first two books are still available."

I grabbed his arm and looked him in the eye. "This is a funeral," I said soberly. "You can't instigate this stuff now."

He scoffed. "Yes, the typist is expressing her moral outrage. Right?" He enunciated the word "typist" and winked at me, but I retained my composure. "No? You don't have anything to share? You sure?" He pulled back his arm.

"Are you alluding to something?" I asked.

"That's the safest possible response to my questions, Janine. I'm impressed."

Seymour was sweating now. "Enough of this!" he yelled. He abruptly moved closer to Simon and a drop of sweat fell on Simon's white shirt. "You have to leave!"

"No!" Simon said defiantly and shook his head violently. His nose nearly collided with Seymour's face. "Absolutely not!" he yelled, moving even closer to Seymour. "She needs to admit her sin to everyone here, once and for all, and you need to admit that Jed's sold more novels since he died than he did in life. You both need to admit these things, because I had a hand in all of it!" He held his hand out and pointed his index finger at us. He waved it as he spoke. "I guided him to that success, and I will no longer be a silent participant!"

"It's on," Yost whispered to me.

"I have nothing to admit," I said. I will never forget that lie. Simon shifted aside to look me in the eye as I expanded on my lie. "You are delusional. I don't know what this is about." I was grasping at straws, but nobody cared because Simon's behavior was so inappropriate.

He flashed a nasty grin and leered at me for a few moments. "Well, there's your ending, Janine," he said bitterly, and then turned back to

Seymour. He persisted hard. "It has sold! You check every hour! Just like he used to! I know that you do it."

Chester Haele finally pushed through the crowd and grabbed him by the arm. "You have to get the fuck out of here right now, Simon." Simon pulled his arm back, and Chester punched him in the jaw. He fell hard and landed on his shoulder with a sharp crunching noise. Chester spit on him. "Motherfucker!"

Juliana Banyon and her mother Tina were nearby. Juliana was a girl Jed knew, and her mom was a fan of the novels. Tina emerged from the others and confronted us. "What was he talking about?" Tina asked.

Simon groaned on the floor. "She has to say it," he said weakly.

I shook my head. "I don't know what he's talking about," I said and left.

I couldn't do it! I couldn't invalidate Jed's success at his own funeral.

From the Journal of Yost Trenko

January 28, 2004

Jed's funeral was bizarre. I spent most of the wake chatting with Janine. Simon instigated quite a ruckus. He argued with Jed's dad and yelled at Janine. Chester beat him up and sprained his shoulder.

I helped Simon up and brought him to the white couch by the window. He recovered rapidly and hadn't broken anything, in spite of the alarming ping that accompanied his fall.

Once he calmed down, I asked him to step outside to talk by the pool with me. "What was that all about, Simon?" I asked.

He bobbed his head fast. "You don't know me very well, but I generally cut to the chase. Sometimes I'm not very diplomatic about it, but that's what I do."

"I've heard that."

"You've seen it too." He paused. "Janine surprised me."

"I went to school with Janine. Did you know that?"

"Yeah."

"She just graduated a semester ahead of me," I said. She's ambitious in her own unique way. I know what your suspicion is, Simon. You think that she was more than just a typist. You think that she delivered a polish that was out of reach for Jed."

"I went to your school too, Yost. I graduated with Jed, and we took the same fiction writing class that you took. I noticed a distinct improvement in the quality of his writing when the novels came out."

"Janine's very good."

"How are you?"

"As a writer?"

He grasped his sore shoulder and winced. "Yeah! What the fuck else? I want to represent writers now."

"What happened to Brook?"

He sighed hard and stared at the pool longingly. "In the New Year, she dropped crystal meth and me. Fuck her." He paused. "Are you any good?"

"No. I'm awful," I said sarcastically.

This did not amuse him at all. Rather, he gave me quite a sour look, and his eyes rapidly widened with rage. "Well, then . . ." His voice was suddenly quite hollow. "Treat this as a polite fuck you, because I despise your bullshit humility." He roughly massaged his bruised shoulder, and snickered at me. "Fucking lightweight!" he yelled with such rage and hatred that I was afraid to explain myself. I think I'm a good writer and would love to have a bulldog like Simon as my agent, but I think that I screwed that up real swell.

From the Journal of Janine

January 29, 2004

I couldn't do it yesterday, but after an uneasy night of sleep, I realized that I ***had*** to do it today. I called Simon this morning and told him everything.

"Why did you tell me all this?"

"Why did you need to know at the funeral yesterday?"

"I like that question. It shows that you finally got smart."

"I know enough about you to realize that all that was about money."

"Yep. I was trolling for writers to represent, and I figured a writer's funeral was a great place to start."

"How clever."

"I knew that I would hear from you. I also think that you did more than you said. For Jed's books. You just admitted a lot, but I think you are holding back more."

"Yes."

"I knew it."

"The schedules he set were always far too ambitious, so I did more and more as it went along. I wrote at least half of the second novel. The third one went south fast, and we fought over it. I had less input on the last one."

"So you've sold yourself short all along?"

"Yes, but I'll never do it again."

"Excellent."

"Jed wrote so much shit!"

"I never really liked Jed. I tolerated him, because he was successful, but his flaky attitude toward the fame pissed me off."

"I agree."

"Good to hear. What about you? Are you any good?"

"Of course."

"Also good to hear. So you're not afraid of success, right?"

"Absolutely not. I want you to sell me."